In Harlequin Presents books seduction and passion are always guaranteed, and this month is no exception! You'll love what we have to offer you this April….

Favorite author Helen Bianchin brings us *The Marriage Possession,* where a devilishly handsome millionaire demands his pregnant mistress marry him. In part two of Sharon Kendrick's enticingly exotic THE DESERT PRINCES trilogy, *The Sheikh's Unwilling Wife,* the son of a powerful desert ruler is determined to make his estranged wife resume her position by his side.

If you love passionate Mediterranean men, then these books will definitely be ones to look out for! In Lynne Graham's *The Italian's Inexperienced Mistress,* an Italian tycoon finds that one night with an innocent English girl just isn't enough! Then in Kate Walker's *Sicilian Husband, Blackmailed Bride,* a sinfully gorgeous Sicilian vows to reclaim his wife in his bed. In *At the Greek Boss's Bidding,* Jane Porter brings you an arrogant Greek billionaire whose temporary blindness leads to an intense relationship with his nurse.

And for all of you who want to be whisked away by a rich man… *The Secret Baby Bargain* by Melanie Milburne tells the story of a ruthless multimillionaire returning to take his ex-fiancée as his wife. In *The Millionaire's Runaway Bride* by Catherine George, the electric attraction between a vulnerable PA and her wealthy ex proves too tempting to resist.

Finally, we have a brand-new author for you! In Abby Green's *Chosen as the Frenchman's Bride* a tall, bronzed Frenchman takes an innocent virgin as his wife. Be sure to look out for more from Abby very soon!

Harlequin Presents®

GREEK TYCOONS

They're the men who have everything—
except brides...

Wealth, power, charm—
what else could a heart-stoppingly handsome
tycoon need? In the GREEK TYCOONS
miniseries you have already been introduced to
some gorgeous Greek multimillionaires who are
in need of wives.

Now it's the turn of talented Harlequin Presents
author Jane Porter, with her romping new
romance *At the Greek Boss's Bidding*.

This tycoon has met his match, and he's decided
he *has* to have her...*whatever* that takes!

Jane Porter

AT THE GREEK BOSS'S BIDDING

GREEK TYCOONS

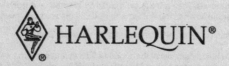

HARLEQUIN®

TORONTO • NEW YORK • LONDON
AMSTERDAM • PARIS • SYDNEY • HAMBURG
STOCKHOLM • ATHENS • TOKYO • MILAN • MADRID
PRAGUE • WARSAW • BUDAPEST • AUCKLAND

ISBN-13: 978-0-373-12623-1
ISBN-10:   0-373-12623-9

AT THE GREEK BOSS'S BIDDING

First North American Publication 2007.

Copyright © 2007 by Jane Porter.

This edition published by arrangement with Harlequin Books S.A.

® and TM are trademarks of the publisher. Trademarks indicated with ® are registered in the United States Patent and Trademark Office, the Canadian Trade Marks Office and in other countries.

www.eHarlequin.com

Printed in U.S.A.

All about the author...
Jane Porter

Born in Visalia, California, I'm a small-town girl at heart. As a little girl I spent hours on my bed, staring out the window, dreaming. In my imagination I was never the geeky bookworm with the thick Coke-bottle glasses, but a princess, a magical fairy, a Joan of Arc crusader.

My parents fed my imagination by taking our family to Europe for a year and overseas I discovered a huge and wonderful world with different cultures and customs. I loved everything about Europe, but felt especially passionate about Italy and those gorgeous Italian men (no wonder my very first Presents hero was Italian).

I confess, after that incredible year in Europe, the travel bug bit, and I spent much of my school years abroad, studying in South Africa, Japan and Ireland.

After my years of traveling and studying I had to settle down and earn a living. With my bachelor degree from UCLA in American studies, I've worked in sales and marketing, as well as a director of a non-profit foundation. Later I earned my master's in writing from the University of San Francisco and taught English.

I now live in rugged Seattle, Washington, with my two young sons. I never mind a rainy day, either, because that's when I sit at my desk and write stories about faraway places, fascinating people and, most importantly of all, love.

Jane loves to hear from her readers. You can write to her at P.O. Box 524, Bellevue, WA 98009, USA.

For two of my favorite heroes: my brothers
Dr. Thomas W. Porter and Robert George Porter.

PROLOGUE

THE helicopter slammed against the rocky incline of the mountain thick with drifts of snow.

Glass shattered, metal crunched and red flames shot from the engine, turning what Kristian Koumantaros knew was glacial white into a shimmering dance of fire and ice.

Unable to see, he struggled with his seatbelt. The helicopter tilted, sliding a few feet. Fire burned everywhere as the heat surged, surrounding him. Kristian tugged his seatbelt again. The clip was jammed.

The smoke seared his lungs, blistering each breath.

Life and death, he thought woozily. Life and death came down to this. And life-and-death decisions were often no different than any other decisions. You did what you had to do and the consequences be damned.

Kristian had done what he had to do and the consequences damned him.

As the roar of the fire grew louder, the helicopter shifted again, the snow giving way.

My God. Kristian threw his arms out, and yet there was nothing to grab, and they were sent tumbling down the mountain face. Another avalanche, he thought, deafened by the endless roar—

And then nothing.

CHAPTER ONE

"*OHI*. No." The deep rough voice could be none other than Kristian Koumantaros himself. "Not interested. Tell her to go away."

Standing in the hall outside the library, Elizabeth Hatchet drew a deep breath, strengthening her resolve. This was not going to be easy, but then nothing about Kristian Koumantaros's case had been easy. Not the accident, not the rehab, not the location of his estate.

It had taken her two days to get here from London—a flight from London to Athens, an endless drive from Athens to Sparta, and finally a bone-jarring cart and donkey trip halfway up the ridiculously inaccessible mountain.

Why anybody, much less a man who couldn't walk and couldn't see, would want to live in a former monastery built on a rocky crag on a slope of Taygetos, the highest mountain in the Peloponnese, was beyond her. But now that she was here, she wasn't going to go away.

"*Kyrios*." Another voice sounded from within the library and Elizabeth recognized the voice as the Greek servant who'd met her at the door. "She's traveled a long way—"

"I've had it with the bloody help from First Class Rehab. First Class, my ass."

Elizabeth closed her eyes and exhaled slowly, counting to ten as she did so.

She'd been told by her Athens staff that it was a long trip to the former monastery.

She'd been warned that reaching rugged Taygetos, with its severe landscape but breathtaking vistas, was nearly as exhausting as caring for Mr. Koumantaros.

Her staff had counseled that traveling up this spectacular mountain with its ancient Byzantine ruins would seem at turns mythical as well as impossible, but Elizabeth, climbing into the donkey cart, had thought she'd been prepared. She'd thought she knew what she was getting into.

Just like she'd thought she knew what she was getting into when she agreed to provide Mr. Koumantaros's home health care after he was released from the French hospital.

In both cases she had been wrong.

The painfully slow, bumpy ride had left her woozy, with a queasy stomach and a pounding headache.

Attempting to rehabilitate Mr. Koumantaros had made her suffer far worse. Quite bluntly, he'd nearly bankrupted her company.

Elizabeth tensed at the sound of glass breaking, followed by a string of select and exceptionally colorful Greek curses.

"*Kyrios,* it's just a glass. It can be replaced."

"I hate this, Pano. Hate everything about this—"

"I know, *kyrios.*" Pano's voice dropped low, and Elizabeth couldn't hear much of what was said, but apparently it had the effect of calming Mr. Koumantaros.

Elizabeth wasn't soothed.

Kristian Koumantaros might be fabulously wealthy and able to afford an eccentric and reclusive lifestyle in the Peloponnese, but that didn't excuse his behavior. And his behavior was nothing short of self-absorbed and self-destructive.

She was here because Kristian Koumantaros couldn't keep a nurse, and he couldn't keep a nurse because he couldn't keep his temper.

The voices in the library were growing louder again. Elizabeth, fluent in Greek, listened as they discussed her.

Mr. Koumantaros didn't want her here.

Pano, the elderly butler, was attempting to convince that Mr. Koumantaros it wouldn't be polite to send the nurse away without seeing her.

Mr. Koumantaros said he didn't care about being polite.

Elizabeth's mouth curved wryly as the butler urged Mr. Koumantaros to at least offer her some refreshment.

Her wry smile disappeared as she heard Mr. Koumantaros answer that as most nurses from First Class Rehab were large women Ms. Hatchet could probably benefit from passing on an afternoon snack.

"*Kyrios*," Pano persisted, "she's brought a suitcase. Luggage. Ms. Hatchet intends to stay."

"*Stay?*" Koumantaros roared.

"Yes, *kyrios.*" The elderly Greek's tone couldn't have been any more apologetic, but his words had the effect of sending Kristian into another litany of curses.

"For God's sake, Pano, leave the damn glass alone and dispense with her. Throw her a bone. Get her a donkey. I don't care. Just do it. *Now.*"

"But she's traveled from London—"

"I don't care if she flew from the moon. She had no business coming here. I left a message two weeks ago with the service. That woman knows perfectly well I've fired them. I didn't ask her to come. And it's not my problem she wasted her time."

Speaking of which, Elizabeth thought, rubbing at the back of her neck to ease the pinch of pain, she *was* wasting time standing here. It was time to introduce herself, get the meeting underway.

Shoulders squared, Elizabeth took a deep breath and pushed the tall door open. As she entered the room, her low heels made a faint clicking sound on the hardwood floor.

"Good afternoon, Mr. Koumantaros," she said. Her narrowed gaze flashed across the shuttered windows, cluttered coffee table, newspapers stacked computer-high on a corner desk. Had to be a month's newspapers piled there, unread.

"You're trespassing, and eavesdropping." Kristian jerked upright in his wheelchair, his deep voice vibrating with fury.

She barely glanced his way, heading instead for the small table filled with prescription bottles. "You were shouting, Mr. Koumantaros. I didn't need to eavesdrop. And I'd be trespassing if your care weren't my responsibility, but it is, so you're going to have to deal with me."

At the table, Elizabeth picked up one of the medicine bottles to check the label, and then the others. It was an old habit, an automatic habit. The first thing a medical professional needed to know was what, if anything, the patient was taking.

Kristian's hunched figure in the wheelchair shuddered as he tried to follow the sound of her movements, his eyes shielded by a white gauze bandage wrapped around his head, the white gauze a brilliant contrast to his thick onyx hair. "Your services have already been terminated," he said tersely.

"You've been overruled," Elizabeth answered, returning the bottles to the table to study him. The bandages swathing his eyes exposed the hard, carved contours of his face. He had chiseled cheekbones, a firm chin and strong jaw shadowed with a rough black beard. From the look of it, he hadn't shaved since the last nurse had been sent packing.

"By whom?" he demanded, leaning crookedly in his chair.

"Your physicians."

"My physicians?"

"Yes, indeed. We're in daily contact with them, Mr. Koumantaros, and these past several months have made them question your mental soundness."

"You must be joking."

"Not at all. There is a discussion that perhaps you'd be better cared for in a facility—"

"Get out!" he demanded, pointing at the door. "Get out now."

Elizabeth didn't move. Instead she cocked her head, coolly examining him. He looked impossibly unkempt, nothing like the sophisticated powerful tycoon he'd reportedly been, with castles and estates scattered all over the world and a gorgeous mistress tucked enticingly in each.

"They fear for you, Mr. Koumantaros," she added quietly, "and so do I. You need help."

"That's absurd. If my doctors were so concerned, they'd be here. And you…you don't know me. You can't drop in here and make assessments based on two minutes of observation."

"I can, because I've managed your case from day one, when you were released from the hospital. No one knows more about you and your day-to-day care than I do. And if you'd always been this despondent we'd see it as a personality issue, but your despair is new—"

"There's no despair. I'm just tired."

"Then let's address that, shall we?" Elizabeth flipped open her leather portfolio and scribbled some notes. One couldn't be too careful these days. She had to protect the agency, not to mention her staff. She'd learned early to document everything. "It's tragic you're still in your present condition— tragic to isolate yourself here on Taygetos when there are people waiting for you in Athens, people wanting you to come home."

"I live here permanently now."

She glanced up at him. "You've no intention of returning?"

"I spent years renovating this monastery, updating and converting it into a modern home to meet my needs."

"That was before you were injured. It's not practical for you to live here now. You can't fly—"

"Don't tell me what I can't do."

She swallowed, tried again. "It's not easy for your friends or family to see you. You're absolutely secluded here—"

"As I wish to be."

"But how can you fully recover when you're so alone in what is undoubtedly one of the most remote places in Greece?"

He averted his head, giving her a glimpse of a very strong, very proud profile. "This is my home," he repeated stubbornly, his tone colder, flintier.

"And what of your company? The businesses? Have you given those up along with your friends and family?"

"If this is your bedside manner—"

"Oh, it is," she assured him unapologetically. "Mr. Koumantaros, I'm not here to coddle you. Nor to say pretty things and try to make you laugh. I'm here to get you on your feet again."

"It's not going to happen."

"Because you like being helpless, or because you're afraid of pain?"

For a moment he said nothing, his face growing paler against the white gauze bandaging his head. Finally he found his voice. "How dare you?" he demanded. "How dare you waltz into my home—?"

"It wasn't exactly a waltz, Mr. Koumantaros. It took me

two days to get here and that included planes, taxis, buses and asses." She smiled thinly. This was the last place she'd wanted to come, and the last person she wanted to nurse. "It's been nearly a year since your accident," she continued. "There's no medical reason for you to be as helpless as you are."

"*Get out.*"

"I can't. Not only have I've nowhere to go—as you must know, it's too dark to take a donkey back down the mountain."

"No, I don't know. I'm blind. I've no idea what time of day it is."

Heat surged to her cheeks. Heat and shame and disgust. Not for her, but him. If he expected her to feel sorry for him, he had another thing coming, and if he hoped to intimidate her, he was wrong again. He could shout and break things, but she wasn't about to cower like a frightened puppy dog. Just because he was a famous Greek with a billion-dollar company didn't mean he deserved her respect. Respect was earned, not automatically given.

"It's almost four o'clock, Mr. Koumantaros. Half of the mountain is already steeped in shadows. I couldn't go home tonight even if I wanted to. Your doctors have authorized me to stay, so I must. It's either that or you go to a rehab facility in Athens. *Your* choice."

"Not much of a choice."

"No, it's not." Elizabeth picked up one of the prescription bottles and popped off the plastic cap to see the number of tablets inside. Three remained from a count of thirty. The prescription had only been refilled a week ago. "Still not sleeping, Mr. Koumantaros?"

"I *can't.*"

"Still in a lot of pain, then?" She pressed the notebook to her chest, stared at him over the portfolio's edge. Probably addicted to his painkillers now. Happened more often than not. One more battle ahead.

Kristian Koumantaros shifted in his wheelchair. The bandages that hid his eyes revealed the sharp twist of his lips. "As if you care."

She didn't even blink. His self-pity didn't trigger sympathy. Self-pity was a typical stage in the healing process—an early stage, one of the first. And the fact that Kristian Koumantaros hadn't moved beyond it meant he had a long, long way to go.

"I do care," she answered flatly. Elizabeth didn't bother to add that she also cared about the future of her company, First Class Rehab, and that providing for Kristian Koumantaros's medical needs had nearly ruined her four-year-old company. "I do care, but I won't be like the others—going soft on you, accepting your excuses, allowing you to get away with murder."

"And what do you know of murder, Miss Holier-Than-Thou?" He wrenched his wheelchair forward, the hard rubber tires crunching glass shards.

"Careful, Mr. Koumantaros! You'll pop a tire."

"*Good.* Pop the goddamn tires. I hate this chair. I hate not seeing. I despise living like this." He swore violently, but at least he'd stopped rolling forward and was sitting still while the butler hurriedly finished sweeping up the glass with a small broom and dustpan.

As Kristian sat, his enormous shoulders turned inward, his dark head hung low.

Despair.

The word whispered to her, summing up what she saw, what she felt. His black mood wasn't merely anger. It was bigger than that, darker than that. His black mood was fed by despair.

He was, she thought, feeling the smallest prick of sympathy, a ruin of a great man.

As swiftly as the sympathy came, she pushed it aside, replacing tenderness with resolve. He'd get well. There was no reason he couldn't.

Elizabeth signaled to Pano that she wanted a word alone with his employer and, nodding, he left them, exiting the library with his dustpan of broken glass.

"Now, then, Mr. Koumantaros," she said as the library doors closed, "we need to get you back on your rehab program. But we can't do that if you insist on intimidating your nurses."

"They were all completely useless, incompetent—"

"All six?" she interrupted, taking a seat on the nearest armchair arm.

He'd gone through the roster of home healthcare specialists in record fashion. In fact, they'd run out of possible candidates. There was no one else to send. And yet Mr. Koumantaros couldn't be left alone. He required more than a butler. He still needed around-the-clock medical care.

"One nurse wasn't so bad. Well, in some ways," he said grudgingly, tapping the metal rim of his wheelchair with his finger tips. "The young one. Calista. And believe me, if she was the best it should show you how bad the others were. But that's another story—"

"Miss Aravantinos isn't coming back." Elizabeth felt her temper rise. Of course he'd request the one nurse he'd broken into bits. The poor girl, barely out of nursing school, had been putty in Kristian Koumantaros's hands. Literally. For a man with life-threatening injuries he'd been incredibly adept at seduction.

His dark head tipped sideways. "Was that her last name?"

"You behaved in a most unscrupulous manner. You're thirty—what?" She quickly flipped through his chart, found his age. "Nearly thirty-six. And she was barely twenty-three. She quit, you know. Left our Athens office. She felt terribly demoralized."

"I never asked Calista to fall in love with me."

"Love?" she choked. "Love didn't have anything to do with it. You seduced her. Out of boredom. And spite."

"You've got me all wrong, Nurse Cratchett—" He paused, a corner of his mouth smirking. "You *are* English, are you not?"

"I speak English, yes," she answered curtly.

"Well, Cratchett, you have me wrong. You see, I'm a lover, not a fighter."

Blood surged to Elizabeth's cheeks. "That's quite enough."

"I've never forced myself on a woman." His voice dropped, the pitch growing deeper, rougher. "If anything, our dear delightful Calista forced herself on me."

"Mr. Koumantaros." Acutely uncomfortable, she gripped her pen tightly, growing warm, warmer. She hated his mocking smile and resented his tone. She could see why Calista had thrown the towel in. How was a young girl to cope with him?

"She romanticized me," he continued, in the same infuriatingly smug vein. "She wanted to know what an invalid was capable of, I suppose. And she discovered that although I can't walk, I can still—"

"Mr. Koumantaros!" Elizabeth jumped to her feet, suddenly oppressed by the warm, dark room. It was late afternoon, and the day had been cloudless, blissfully sunny. She couldn't fathom why the windows and shutters were all closed, keeping the fresh mountain air out. "I do not wish to hear the details."

"But you need them." Kristian pushed his wheelchair toward her, blue cotton sleeves rolled back on his forearms, corded tendons tight beneath his skin. He'd once had a very deep tan, but the tan had long ago faded. His olive skin was pale, testament to his long months indoors. "You're misinformed if you think I took advantage of Calista. Calista got what Calista wanted."

She averted her head and ground her teeth together. "She was a wonderful, promising young nurse."

"I don't know about wonderful, but I'll give you naïve. And since she quit, I think you've deliberately assigned me nurses from hell."

"We do not employ nurses from hell. All of our nurses are professional, efficient, compassionate—"

"And stink to high heaven."

"Excuse me?" Elizabeth drew back, affronted. "That's a crude accusation."

"Crude, but true. And I didn't want them in my home, and I refused to have them touching me."

So that was it. He didn't want a real nurse. He wanted something from late-night T.V.—big hair, big breasts, and a short, tight skirt.

Elizabeth took a deep breath, fighting to hang on to her professional composure. She was beginning to see how he wore his nurses down, brow-beating and tormenting until they begged for a reprieve. *Anyone but Mr. Koumantaros. Any job but that!*

Well, she wasn't about to let Mr. Koumantaros break her. He couldn't get a rise out of her because she wouldn't let him. "Did Calista smell bad?"

"No, Calista smelled like heaven."

For a moment she could have sworn Kristian was smiling, and the fact that he could smile over ruining a young nurse's career infuriated her.

He rolled another foot closer. "But then after Calista fled you sent only old, fat, frumpy nurses to torture me, punishing me for what was really Calista's fault. And don't tell me they weren't old and fat and frumpy, because I might be blind but I'm not stupid."

Elizabeth's blood pressure shot up again. "I assigned mature nurses, but they were well-trained and certainly prepared for the rigors of the job."

"One smelled like a tobacco shop. One of fish. I'm quite certain another could have been a battleship—"

"You're being insulting."

"I'm being honest. You replaced Calista with prison guards."

Elizabeth's anger spiked, and then her lips twitched. Kristian Koumantaros was actually right.

After poor Calista's disgrace, Elizabeth had intentionally assigned Mr. Koumantaros only the older, less responsive nurses, realizing that he required special care. Very special care.

She smiled faintly, amused despite herself. He might not be walking, and he might not have his vision, but his brain worked just fine.

Still smiling, she studied him dispassionately, aware of his injuries, his months of painful rehabilitation, his prognosis. He was lucky to have escaped such a serious accident with his life. The trauma to his head had been so extensive he'd been expected to suffer severe brain damage. Happily, his mental faculties were intact. His motor skills could be repaired, but his eyesight was questionable. Sometimes the brain healed itself. Sometimes it didn't. Only time and continued therapy would tell.

"Well, that's all in the past now," she said, forcing a note of cheer into her voice. "The battleaxe nurses are gone. I am here—"

"And you are probably worse than all of them."

"Indeed, I am. They whisper behind my back that I'm every patient's worst nightmare."

"So I can call you Nurse Cratchett, then?"

"If you'd like. Or you can call me by my name, which is Nurse Hatchet. But they're so similar, I'll answer either way."

He sat in silence, his jaw set, his expression increasingly wary. Elizabeth felt the edges of her mouth lift, curl. He couldn't browbeat or intimidate her. She knew what Greek tycoons were. She'd once been married to one.

"It's time to move on," she added briskly. "And the first place we start is with your meals. I know it's late, Mr. Koumantaros, but have you eaten lunch yet?"

"I'm not hungry."

Elizabeth closed her portfolio and slipped the pen into the leather case. "You need to eat. Your body needs the nutrition. I'll see about a light meal." She moved toward the door, unwilling to waste time arguing.

Kristian shoved his wheelchair forward, inadvertently slamming into the edge of the couch. His frustration was written in every line of his face. "I don't want food—"

"Of course not. Why eat when you're addicted to pain pills?" She flashed a tight, strained smile he couldn't see. "Now, if you'll excuse me, I'll see to your meal."

The vaulted stone kitchen was in the tower, or *pyrgos,* and there the butler, cook and senior housekeeper had gathered beneath one of the medieval arches. They were in such deep conversation that they didn't hear Elizabeth enter.

Once they realized she was there, all three fell silent and turned to face her with varying degrees of hostility.

Elizabeth wasn't surprised. For one, unlike the other nurses, she wasn't Greek. Two, despite being foreign, she spoke Greek fluently. And three, she wasn't showing proper deference to their employer, a very wealthy, powerful Greek man.

"Hello," Elizabeth said, attempting to ignore the icy

welcome. "I thought I'd see if I could help with Mr. Koumantaros's lunch."

Everyone continued to gape at her until Pano, the butler, cleared his throat. "Mr. Koumantaros doesn't eat lunch."

"Does he take a late breakfast, then?" Elizabeth asked.

"No, just coffee."

"Then when does he eat his first meal?"

"Not until evening."

"I see." Elizabeth's brow furrowed as she studied the three staffers, wondering how long they'd been employed by Kristian Koumantaros and how they coped with his black moods and display of temper. "Does he eat well then?"

"Sometimes," the short, stocky cook answered, wiping her hands across the starched white fabric of her apron. "And sometimes he just pecks. He used to have an excellent appetite—fish, *moussaka, dolmades,* cheese, meat, vegetables—but that was before the accident."

Elizabeth nodded, glad to see at least one of them had been with him a while. That was good. Loyalty was always a plus, but misplaced loyalty could also be a hindrance to Kristian recovering. "We'll have to improve his appetite," she said. "Starting with a light meal right now. Perhaps a *horiatiki salata,*" she said, suggesting what most Europeans and Americans thought of as a Greek salad—feta cheese and onion, tomato and cucumber, drizzled with olive oil and a few drops of homemade wine vinegar.

"There must be someplace outside—a sunny terrace— where he can enjoy his meal. Mr. Koumantaros needs the sun and fresh air—"

"Excuse me, ma'am," Pano interrupted, "but the sun bothers Mr. Koumantaros's eyes."

"It's because Mr. Koumantaros has spent too much time

sitting in the dark. The light will do him good. Sunlight stimulates the pituitary gland, helps alleviate depression and promotes healing. But, seeing as he's been inside so much, we can transition today by having lunch in the shade. I assume part of the terrace is covered?"

"Yes, ma'am," the cook answered. "But Mr. Koumantaros won't go."

"Oh, he will." Elizabeth swallowed, summoning all her determination. She knew Kristian would eventually go. But it'd be a struggle.

Sitting in the library, Kristian heard the English nurse's footsteps disappear as she went in search of the kitchen, and after a number of long minutes heard her footsteps return.

So she was coming back. Wonderful.

He tipped his head, looking up at nothing, since everything was and had been dark since the crash, fourteen months and eleven days ago.

The door opened, and he knew from the way the handle turned and the lightness of the step that it was her. "You're wrong about something else," he said abruptly as she entered the library. "The accident wasn't a year ago. It was almost a year and a half ago. It happened late February."

She'd stopped walking and he felt her there, beyond his sight, beyond his reach, standing, staring, *waiting*. It galled him, this lack of knowing, seeing. He'd achieved what he'd achieved by utilizing his eyes, his mind, his gut. He trusted his eyes and his gut, and now, without those, he didn't know what was true, or real.

Like Calista, for example.

"That's even worse," his new nightmare nurse shot back. "You should be back at work by now. You've a corporation to run, people dependent on you. You're doing no one any good hiding away here in your villa."

"I can't run my company if I can't walk or see—"

"But you *can* walk, and there might be a chance you could see—"

"A less than five percent chance." He laughed bitterly. "You know, before the last round of surgeries I had a thirty-five percent chance of seeing, but they botched those—"

"They weren't botched. They were just highly experimental."

"Yes, and that experimental treatment reduced my chances of seeing again to nil."

"Not nil."

"Five percent. There's not much difference. Especially when they say that even if the operation were a success I'd still never be able to drive, or fly, or sail. That there's too much trauma for me to do what I used to do."

"And your answer is to sit here shrouded in bandages and darkness and feel sorry for yourself?" she said tartly, her voice growing closer.

Kristian shifted in his chair, and felt an active and growing dislike for Cratchett. She was standing off to his right, and her smug, superior attitude rubbed him the wrong way. "Your company's services have been terminated."

"They haven't—"

"I may be blind, but you're apparently deaf. First Class Rehab has received its last—*final*—check. There is no more coming from me. There will be no more payments for services rendered."

He heard her exhale—a soft, quick breath that was so uniquely feminine that he drew back, momentarily startled.

And in that half-second he felt betrayed.

She was the one not listening. She was the one forcing herself on him. And yet—and yet she was a woman. And he was—or had been—a gentleman, and gentlemen were supposed to have manners. Gentlemen were supposed to be above reproach.

Growling, he leaned back in his chair, gripped the rims on the wheels and glared at where he imagined her to be standing.

He shouldn't feel bad for speaking bluntly. His brow furrowed even more deeply. It was her fault. She'd come here, barging in with a righteous high-handed, bossy attitude that turned his stomach.

The accident hadn't been yesterday. He'd lived like this long enough to know what he was dealing with. He didn't need her telling him this and that, as though he couldn't figure it out for himself.

No, she—Nurse Hatchet-Cratchett, his nurse number seven—had the same bloody mentality as the first six. In their eyes the wheelchair rendered him incompetent, unable to think for himself.

"I'm not paying you any longer," he repeated firmly, determined to get this over and done with. "You've had your last payment. You and your company are finished here."

And then she made that sound again—that little sound which had made him draw back. But this time he recognized the sound for what it was.

A laugh.

She was laughing at him.

Laughing and walking around the side of his chair so he had to crane his head to try to follow her.

He felt her hands settle on the back of his chair. She must have bent down, or perhaps she wasn't very tall, because her voice came surprisingly close to his ear.

"But *you* aren't paying me any longer. Our services have been retained and we are authorized to continue providing your care. Only now, instead of you paying for your care, the financial arrangements are being handled by a private source."

He went cold—cold and heavy. Even his legs, with their only limited sensation. *"What?"*

"It's true," she continued, beginning to push his chair and moving him forward. "I'm not the only one who thinks its high time you recovered." She continued pushing him despite his attempt to resist. "You're going to get well," she added, her voice whispering sweetly in his ear. "Whether you want to or not."

CHAPTER TWO

KRISTIAN clamped down on the wheel-rims, holding them tight to stop their progress. "Who is paying for my care?"

Elizabeth hated played games, and she didn't believe it was right to keep anyone in the dark, but she'd signed a confidentiality agreement and she had to honor it. "I'm sorry, Mr. Koumantaros. I'm not at liberty to say."

Her answer only antagonized him further. Kristian threw his head back and his powerful shoulders squared. His hands gripped the rims so tightly his knuckles shone white. "I won't have someone else assuming responsibility for my care, much less for what is surely questionable care."

Elizabeth cringed at the criticism. The criticism—slander?—was personal. It was her company. She personally interviewed, hired and trained each nurse that worked for First Class Rehab. Not that he knew. And not that she wanted him to know right now.

No, what mattered now was getting Mr. Koumantaros on a schedule, creating a predictable routine with regular periods of nourishment, exercise and rest. And to do that she really needed him to have his lunch.

"We can talk more over lunch," Elizabeth replied, beginning to roll him back out onto the terrace once more. But, just like before, Kristian clamped his hands down and gripped the wheel-rims hard, preventing him from going forward.

"I don't like being pushed."

Elizabeth stepped away and stared down at him, seeing for the first time the dark pink scar that snaked from beneath the sleeve of his sky-blue Egyptian cotton shirt, running from elbow to wrist. A multiple fracture, she thought, recalling just how many bones had broken. By all indications he should have died. But he hadn't. He'd survived. And after all that she wasn't about to let him give up now and wither away inside this shuttered villa.

"I didn't think you could get yourself around," she said, hanging on to her patience by a thread.

"I can push myself short distances."

"That's not quite the same thing as walking, is it?" she said exasperatedly. If he could do more…if he could walk…why didn't he? *Ornio,* she thought, using the Greek word for ornery. The previous nurses hadn't exaggerated a bit. Kristian was as obstinate as a mule.

He snorted. "Is that your idea of encouragement?"

Her lips compressed. Kristian also knew how to play both sides. One minute he was the aggressor, the next the victim. Worse, he was succeeding in baiting her, getting to her, and no one ever—*ever*—got under her skin. Not anymore. "It's a statement of fact, Mr. Koumantaros. You're still in the chair because your muscles have atrophied since the accident. But initially the doctors expected you to walk again." *They thought you'd want to.*

"It didn't work out."

"Because it hurt too much?"

"The therapy wasn't working."

"You gave up." She reached for the handles on the back of his chair and gave a hard push. "Now, how about that lunch?"

He wouldn't release the rims. "How about you tell me who is covering your services, and then we'll have lunch?"

Part of her admired his bargaining skill and tactics. He was clearly a leader, and accustomed to being in control. But she was a leader, too, and she was just as comfortable giving direction. "I can't tell you." Her jaw firmed. "Not until you're walking."

He craned to see her, even though he couldn't see anything. "So you *can* tell me."

"Once you're walking."

"Why not until then?"

She shrugged. "It's the terms of the contract."

"But you know this person?"

"We spoke on the phone."

He grew still, his expression changing as well, as though he were thinking, turning inward. "How long until I walk?"

"It depends entirely on you. Your hamstrings and hip muscles have unfortunately tightened, shortening up, but it's not irreparable, Mr. Koumantaros. It just requires diligent physical therapy."

"But even with *diligent* therapy I'll always need a walker."

She heard his bitterness but didn't comment on it. It wouldn't serve anything at this point. "A walker or a cane. But isn't that better than a wheelchair? Wouldn't you enjoy being independent again?"

"But it'll never be the same, never as it was—"

"People are confronted by change every day, Mr. Koumantaros."

"Do not patronize me." His voice deepened, roughened, revealing blistering fury.

"I'm not trying to. I'm trying to understand. And if this is because others died and you—"

"Not one more word," he growled. "Not one."

"Mr. Koumantaros, you are no less of a man because others died and you didn't."

"Then you do not know me. You do not know who I am, or who I was before. Because the best part of me—the good in me—died that day on the mountain. The good in me perished while I was saving someone I didn't even like."

He laughed harshly, the laugh tinged with self-loathing. "I'm not a hero. I'm a monster." And, reaching up, with a savage yank he ripped the bandages from his head. Rearing back in his wheelchair, Kristian threw his head into sunlight. "Do you see the monster now?"

Elizabeth sucked in her breath as the warm Mediterranean light touched the hard planes of his face.

A jagged scar ran the length of the right side of his face, ending precariously close to his right eye. The skin was still a tender pink, although one day it would pale, lightening until it nearly matched his skin tone—as long as he stayed out of the sun.

But the scar wasn't why she stared. And the scar wasn't what caused her chest to seize up, squeezing with a terrible, breathless tenderness.

Kristian Koumantaros was beautiful. Beyond beautiful. Even with the scar snaking like a fork of lightning over his cheekbone, running from the corner of his mouth to the edge of his eye.

"God gave me a face to match my heart. Finally the outside and inside look the same," he gritted, hands convulsing in his lap.

"You're wrong." Elizabeth could hardly breathe. His words gave her so much pain, so much sorrow, she felt tears sting her eyes. "If God gave you a face to match your heart, your heart is beautiful, too. Because a scar doesn't ruin a face, and a scar doesn't ruin a heart. It just shows that you've lived—" she took a rough breath "—and loved."

He said nothing and she pressed on. "Besides, I think the scar suits you. You were too good-looking before."

For a split second he said nothing, and then he laughed, a fierce guttural laugh that was more animal-like than human. "Finally. Someone to tell me the truth."

Elizabeth ignored the pain pricking her insides, the stab of more pain in her chest. Something about him, something about this—the scarred face, the shattered life, the fury, the fire, the intelligence and passion—touched her. Hurt her. It was not that anyone should suffer, but somehow on Kristian the suffering became bigger, larger than life, a thing in and of itself.

"You're an attractive man even with the scar," she said, still kneeling next to his chair.

"It's a hideous scar. It runs the length of my face. I can feel it."

"You're quite vain, then, Mr. Koumantaros?"

His head swung around and the expression on his face, matched by the cloudiness in his deep blue eyes, stole her breath. *He didn't suit the chair.*

Or the chair didn't suit him. He was too big, too strong, too much of everything. And it was wrong, his body, his life, his personality contained by it. Confined to it.

"No man wants to feel like Frankenstein," Kristian said with another rough laugh.

She knew then that it wasn't his face that made him feel so broken, but his heart and mind. Those memories of his that haunted him, the flashes of the past that made him relive the accident over and over. She knew because she'd once been the same. She, too, had relived an accident in endless detail, stopping the mental camera constantly, freezing the lens at the first burst of flame and the final ball of fire. But that was her story, not his, and she couldn't allow her own experiences and emotions to cloud her judgment now.

She had to regain some control, retreat as quickly as possible to professional detachment. She wasn't here for him; she was here for a job. She wasn't his love interest. He had one in Athens, waiting for him to recover. It was this lover of his who'd insisted he walk, he function, he see, and that was why she was here. To help him recover. To help him return to her.

"You're far from Frankenstein," she said crisply, covering her suddenly ambivalent emotions. She rose to her feet, smoothed her straight skirt and adjusted her blouse. "But, since you require flattery, let me give it to you. The scar suits you. Gives your face character. Makes you look less like a model or a movie star and more like a man."

"A man," he repeated with a bitter laugh.

"Yes, a man. And with some luck and hard work, soon we'll have you acting like a man, too."

Chaotic emotions rushed across his face. Surprise, then confusion, and as she watched the confusion shifted into anger. She'd caught him off guard and hurt him. She could see she'd hurt him.

Swallowing the twinge of guilt, she felt it on the tip of her tongue to apologize, as she hadn't meant to hurt his feelings so much as provoke him into taking action.

But even as she attempted to put a proper apology together, she sensed anything she said, particularly anything sympathetic, would only antagonize him more. He was living in his own hell.

More gently she added, "You've skied the most inaccessible mountain faces in the world, piloted helicopters in blizzards, rescued a half-dozen—"

"Enough."

"You can do anything," she persisted. His suffering was so obvious it was criminal. She'd become a nurse to help those wounded, not to inflict fresh wounds, but sometimes patients were so overwhelmed by physical pain and mental misery that they self-destructed.

Brilliant men—daring, risk-taking, gifted men—were particularly vulnerable, and she'd learned the hard way that these same men self-destructed if they had no outlet for their anger, no place for their pain.

Elizabeth vowed to find the outlet for Kristian, vowed she'd channel his fury somehow, turning pain into positives.

And so, before he could speak, before he could give voice to any of his anger, or contradict her again, she mentioned the pretty table setting before them, adding that the cook and butler had done a superb job preparing their late lunch.

"Your staff have outdone themselves, Mr. Koumantaros. They've set a beautiful table on your terrace. Can you feel that breeze? You can smell the scent of pine in the warm air."

"I don't smell it."

"Then come here, where I'm standing. It really is lovely. You can get a whiff of the herbs in your garden, too. Rosemary, and lemongrass."

But he didn't roll forward. He rolled backward, retreating back toward the shadows. "It's too bright. The light makes my head hurt."

"Even if I replace the bandages?"

"Even with the bandages." His voice grew harsh, pained. "And I don't want lunch. I already told you that but you don't listen. You won't listen. No one does."

"We could move lunch inside—"

"*I don't want lunch.*" And with a hard push he disappeared into the cooler library, where he promptly bumped into a side-table and sent it crashing, which led to him cursing and another bang of furniture.

Tensing, Elizabeth fought the natural inclination to hurry and help him. She wanted to rush to his side, but knew that doing so would only prolong his helpless state. She couldn't become an enabler, couldn't allow him to continue as he'd done—retreating from life, retreating from living, retreating into the dark shadows of his mind.

Instead, with nerves of steel, she left him as he was, muttering and cursing and banging into the table he'd overturned, and headed slowly across the terrace to the pretty lunch table, with its cheerful blue and white linens and cluster of meadow flowers in the middle.

And while she briefly appreciated the pretty linens and fresh flowers, she forgot both just as quickly, her thoughts focused on one thing and only one—Kristian Koumantaros.

It had cost her to speak to him so bluntly. She'd never been this confrontational—she'd never needed to be until now—but, frankly, she didn't know what else to do with him at this point. Her agency had tried everything—they'd sent every capable nurse, attempted every course of therapy—all to no avail.

As Elizabeth gratefully took a seat at the table, she knew her exhaustion wasn't just caused by Kristian's obstinance, but by Kristian himself.

Kristian had gotten beneath her skin.

And it's not his savage beauty, she told herself sternly. It couldn't be. She wasn't so superficial as to be moved by the violence in his face and frame—although he had an undeniably handsome face. So what was it? Why did she feel horrifyingly close to tears?

Ignoring the nervous flutter in her middle, she unfolded her linen serviette and spread it across her lap.

Pano appeared, a bottle of bubbling mineral water in his hand. "Water, ma'am?"

"Please, Pano. Thank you."

"And is Mr. Koumantaros joining you?"

She glanced toward the library doors, which had just been shut. She felt a weight on her heart, and the weight seemed to swell and grow. "No, Pano, not today. Not after all."

He filled her glass. "Shall I take him a plate?"

Elizabeth shot another glance toward the closed and shuttered library doors. She hesitated but a moment. "No. We'll try again tonight at dinner."

"So nothing if he asks?" The butler sounded positively pained.

"I know it seems hard, but I must somehow reach him. I must make him respond. He can't hide here forever. He's too young, and there are too many people that love him and miss him."

Pano seemed to understand this. His bald head inclined and, with a polite, "Your luncheon will be served immediately," he disappeared, after leaving the mineral water bottle on the table within her reach.

One of the villa's younger staff served the lunch—*souvlaki,* with sliced cucumbers and warm fresh pitta. It wasn't the meal she'd requested, and Elizabeth suspected it was intentional, the cook's own rebellion, but at least a meal had been prepared.

Elizabeth didn't eat immediately, choosing to give Kristian time in case he changed his mind. Brushing a buzzing fly away, she waited five minutes, and then another five more, reflecting that she hadn't gotten off to the best start here. It had been bumpy in more ways than one. But she could only press on, persevere. Everything would work out. Kristian Koumantaros would walk again, and eventually return to Athens, where he'd resume responsibility for the huge corporation he owned and had once single-handedly run. She'd go home to England and be rid of Greece and Greek tycoons.

After fifteen minutes Elizabeth gave up the vigil. Kristian wasn't coming. Finally she ate, concentrating on savoring the excellent meal and doing her best to avoid thinking about the next confrontation with her mulish patient.

Lunch finished, Elizabeth wiped her mouth on her serviette and pushed away from the table. Time to check on Kristian.

In the darkened library, Kristian lifted his head as she entered the room. "Have a nice lunch?" he asked in terse Greek.

She winced at the bitterness in his voice. "Yes, thank you. You have an excellent cook."

"Did you enjoy the view?"

"It is spectacular," she agreed, although she'd actually spent most of the time thinking about him instead of the view. She hadn't felt this involved with any case in years. But then, she hadn't nursed anyone directly in years, either.

After her stint in nursing school, and then three years working at a regional hospital, she'd gone back to school and earned her Masters in Business Administration, with an emphasis on Hospital and Medical Administration. After graduating she had immediately found work. So much work she had realized she'd be better off working for herself than anyone else—which was how her small, exclusive First Class Rehab had been born.

But Kristian Koumantaros's case was special. Kristian Koumantaros hadn't improved in her company's care. He'd worsened.

And to Elizabeth it was completely unacceptable.

Locating her notebook on the side-table, where she'd left it earlier, she took a seat on the couch. "Mr. Koumantaros, I know you don't want a nurse, but you still need one. In fact, you need several."

"Why not prescribe a fleet?" he asked sarcastically.

"I think I shall." She flipped open her brown leather portfolio and, scanning her previous notes, began to scribble again. "A live-in nursing assistant to help with bathing, personal hygiene. Male, preferably. Someone strong to lift you in and out of your chair since you're not disposed to walk."

"I can't walk, Mrs.—"

"*Ms.* Hatchet," she supplied, before crisply continuing, "And you could walk if you had worked with your last four physical therapists. They all tried, Mr. Koumantaros, but you were more interested in terrifying them than in making progress."

Elizabeth wrote another couple of notes, then clicked her pen closed. "You also require an occupational therapist, as you desperately need someone to adapt your lifestyle. If you've no intention of getting better, your house and habits will need to change. Ramps, a second lift, a properly outfitted bathroom, rails and grabs in the pool—"

"No," he thundered, face darkening. "No bars, no rails, and no goddamn grabs in this house."

She clicked her pen open again. "Perhaps its time we called in a psychiatrist—someone to evaluate your depression and recommend a course of therapy. Pills, perhaps, or sessions of counseling."

"I will never talk—"

"You are now," she said cheerfully, scribbling yet another note to herself, glancing at Kristian Koumantaros from beneath her lashes. His jaw was thick, and rage was stiffening his spine, improving his posture, curling his hands into fists.

Good, she thought, with a defiant tap of her pen. He hadn't given up on living, just given up on healing. There was something she—and her agency—could still do.

She watched him for a long dispassionate moment.

"Talking—counseling—will help alleviate your depression, and it's depression that's keeping you from recovering."

"I'm not depressed."

"Then someone to treat your rage. You *are* raging, Mr. Koumantaros. Are you aware of your tone?"

"*My* tone?" He threw himself back in his chair, hands flailing against the rims of the wheels, furious skin against steel. "*My* tone? You come into my house and lecture me about my tone? Who the hell do you think you are?"

The raw savagery in his voice cut her more than his words, and for a moment the library spun. Elizabeth held her breath, silent, stunned.

"You think you're so good." Kristian's voice sounded from behind her, mocking her. "So righteous, so sure of everything. But would you be so sure of yourself if the rug was pulled from beneath *your* feet? Would you be so callous then?"

Of course he didn't know the rug *had* been pulled from beneath her feet. No one got through life unscathed. But her personal tragedies had toughened her, and she thought of the old wounds as scar tissue...something that was just part of her.

Even so, Elizabeth felt a moment of gratitude that Kristian couldn't see her, or the conflicting emotions flickering over her face. Hers wasn't a recent loss, hers was seven years ago, and yet if she wasn't careful to keep up the defenses the loss still felt as though it had happened yesterday.

As the silence stretched Kristian laughed low, harshly. "I got you on that one." His laughter deepened, and then abruptly ended. "Hard to sit in judgment until you've walked a mile in someone else's shoes."

Through the open doors Elizabeth could hear the warble of a bird, and she wondered if it was the dark green bird, the one with the lemon-yellow breast, she'd seen while eating on the patio terrace.

"I'm not as callous as you think," she said, her voice cool enough to contradict her words. "But I'm here to help you, and I'll do whatever I must to see you move into the next step of recovery."

"And why should I want to recover?" His head angled, and his expression was ferocious. "And don't give me some sickly-sweet answer about finding my true love and having a family and all that nonsense."

Elizabeth's lips curved in a faint, hard smile. No, she'd never dangle love as a motivational tool, because even that could be taken away. "I wasn't. You should know by now that's not my style."

"So tell me? Give it to me straight? Why should I bother to get better?"

Why bother? Why bother, indeed? Elizabeth felt her heart race—part anger, part sympathy. "Because you're still alive, that's why."

"That's it?" Kristian laughed bitterly. "Sorry, that's not much incentive."

"Too bad," she answered, thinking she *was* sorry about his accident, but he wasn't dead.

Maybe he couldn't walk easily or see clearly, but he was still intact and he had his life, his heart, his body, his mind. Maybe he wasn't exactly as he had been before the injury, but that didn't make him less of a man…not unless he let it. And he was allowing it.

Pressing the tip of her finger against her mouth, she fought to hold back all the angry things she longed to say, knowing she wasn't here to judge. He was just a patient, and her job was to provide medical care, not morality lessons. But, even acknowledging that it wasn't her place to criticize, she felt her tension grow.

Despite her best efforts, she resented his poor-me attitude, was irritated that he was so busy looking at the small picture he was missing the big one. Life was so precious. Life was a gift, not a right, and he still possessed the gift.

He could love and be loved. Fall in love, make love, shower someone with affection—hugs, kisses, tender touches. There was no reason he couldn't make someone feel cherished, important, unforgettable. No reason other than that he didn't want to, that he'd rather feel sorry for himself than reach out to another.

"Because, for whatever reason, Mr. Koumantaros, you're still here with us, still alive. Don't look a gift horse in the mouth. Live. Live fully, wisely. And if you can't do it for yourself, then do it for those who didn't escape the avalanche that day with you." She took a deep breath. "Do it for Cosima. Do it for Andreas."

CHAPTER THREE

COSIMA and Andreas. Kristian was surprised his English Nurse Cratchett knew their names, as it was Cosima and Andreas who haunted him. And for very different reasons.

Kristian shifted restlessly in bed. His legs ached at the moment. Sometimes the pain was worse than others, and it was intense tonight. Nothing made him comfortable.

The accident. A winter holiday with friends and family in the French Alps.

He'd been in a coma for weeks after the accident, and when he'd come out of it he'd been immobilized for another couple weeks to give his spine a chance to heal. He'd been told he was lucky there was no lasting paralysis, told he was lucky to have survived such a horrific accident.

But for Kristian the horror continued. And it wasn't even his eyes he missed, or his strength. It was Andreas, Andreas—not just his big brother, but his best friend.

And while he and Andreas had always been about the extreme—extreme skiing, extreme diving, extreme parasailing—Andreas, the eldest, had been the straight arrow, as good as the sun, while Kristian had played the bad boy and rebel.

Put them together—fair-haired Andreas and devilish Kristian—and they'd been unstoppable. They'd had too much damn fun. Not that they hadn't worked—they'd worked hard—but they had played even harder.

It had helped that they were both tall, strong, physical. They'd practically grown up on skis, and Kristian couldn't even remember a time when he and Andreas hadn't participated in some ridiculous, reckless thrill-seeking adventure. Their father, Stavros, had been an avid sportsman, and their stunning French mother hadn't been just beautiful, she'd once represented France in the Winter Olympics. Sport had been the family passion.

Of course there had been dangers, but their father had taught them to read mountains, study weather reports, discuss snow conditions with avalanche experts. They'd coupled their love of adventure with intelligent risk-taking. And, so armed, they had embraced life.

And why shouldn't they have? They'd been part of a famous, wealthy, powerful family. Money and opportunity had never been an issue.

But money and opportunity didn't protect one from tragedy. It didn't insure against heartbreak or loss.

Andreas was the reason Kristian needed the pills. Andreas was the reason he couldn't sleep.

Why hadn't he saved his brother first? Why had he waited?

Kristian stirred yet again, his legs alive and on fire. The doctors said it was nerves and tissue healing, but the pain was maddening. Felt like licks of lightning everywhere.

Kristian searched the top of his bedside table for medicine but found nothing. His nurse must have taken the pain meds he always kept there.

If only he could sleep.

If he could just relax maybe the pain would go away. But he wasn't relaxing, and he needed something—anything—to take his mind off the accident and what had happened that day on Le Meije.

There had been ten of them who had set off together for a final run. They'd been heli-skiing all week, and it had been their next to last day. Conditions had looked good, the ski guides had given the okay, and the helicopter had taken off. Less than two hours later, only three of their group survived.

Cosima had lived, but not Andreas.

Kristian had saved Cosima instead of his brother, and that was the decision that tormented him.

Kristian had never even liked Cosima—not even at their first meeting. From the very beginning she'd struck him as a shallow party girl who lived for the social scene, and nothing she'd said or done during the next two years had convinced him otherwise. Of course Andreas had never seen that side in her. He'd only seen her beauty, her style, and her fun—and maybe she was beautiful, stylish, but Andreas could have done better.

Driven to find relief, Kristian searched the table-top again, before painfully rolling over onto his stomach to reach into the small drawers, in case the bottles had been put there. Nothing.

Then he remembered the bottle tucked between the mattresses, and was just reaching for it when his bedroom door opened and he heard the click of a light switch on the wall.

"You're still awake." It was dear old Cratchett, on her night rounds.

"Missing the hospital routine?" he drawled, slowly rolling onto his back and dragging himself into a sitting position.

Elizabeth approached the bed. "I haven't worked in a hospital in years. My company specializes in private home healthcare."

He listened to her footsteps, trying to imagine her age. He'd played this game with all the nurses. Since he couldn't see, he created his own visual images. And, listening to Elizabeth Hatchet's voice and footsteps, he began to create a mental picture of her.

Age? Thirty-something. Maybe close to forty.

Brunette, redhead, black-haired or blonde?

She leaned over the bed and he felt her warmth even as he caught a whiff of a light fresh scent—the same crisp, slightly sweet fragrance he'd smelled earlier. Not exactly citrus, and not hay—possibly grass? Fresh green grass. With sunshine. But also rain.

"Can't sleep?" she asked, and her voice sounded tantalizingly near.

"I never sleep."

"In pain?"

"My legs are on fire."

"You need to use them, exercise them. It'd improve circulation and eventually alleviate most of the pain symptoms you're experiencing."

For a woman with such a brusque bedside manner she had a lovely voice. The tone and pitch reminded him of the string section of the orchestra. Not a cello or bass, but a violin. Warm, sweet, evocative.

"You sound so sure of yourself," he said, hearing her move again, sensing her closeness.

"This is my job. It's what I do," she said. "And tell me, Mr. Koumantaros, what do *you* do—besides throw yourself down impossibly vertical slopes?"

"You don't approve of extreme skiing?"

Elizabeth felt her chest grow tight. Extreme skiing. Jumping off mountains. Dodging avalanches. It was ridiculous—ridiculous to tempt fate like that.

Impatiently she tugged the sheets and coverlet straight at the foot of the bed, before smoothing the covers with a jerk on the sheet at its edge.

"I don't approve of risking life for sport," she answered. "No."

"But sport is exercise—and isn't that what you're telling me I must do?"

She looked down at him, knowing he was attempting to bait her once again. He wasn't wearing a shirt, and his chest was big, his shoulders immense. She realized that this was all just a game to him, like his love of sport.

He wanted to push her—had pushed her nurses, pushed all of them. Trying to distract them from doing their job was a form of entertainment for him, a diversion to keep him from facing the consequences of his horrific accident.

"Mr. Koumantaros, there are plenty of exercises that don't risk life or limb—or cost an exorbitant amount of money."

"Is it the sport or the money you object to, Nurse?"

"Both," she answered firmly.

"How refreshing. An Englishwoman with an opinion on everything."

Once again she didn't rise to the bait. She knew he must be disappointed, too. Maybe he'd been able to torment his other nurses, but he wouldn't succeed in torturing her.

She had a job to do, and she'd do it, and then she'd go home and life would continue—far more smoothly once she had Kristian Koumantaros out of it.

"Your pillows," she said, her voice as starchy as the white blouse tucked into cream slacks. Her only bit of ornamentation was the slender gold belt at her waist.

She'd thought she'd given him ample warning that she was about to lean over and adjust his pillows, but as she reached across him he suddenly reached up toward her and his hand became entangled in her hair.

She quickly stepped back, flustered. She'd heard all about Kristian's playboy antics, knew his reputation was that of a lady's man, but she was dumbfounded that he'd still try to pull that on her. "Without being able to see, you didn't realize I was there," she said coolly, wanting to avoid all allegations of improper conduct. "In the future I will ask you to move before I adjust your pillows or covers."

"It was just your hair," he said mildly. "It brushed my face. I was merely moving it out of the way."

"I'll make sure to wear it pulled back tomorrow."

"Your hair is very long."

She didn't want to get into the personal arena. She already felt exceedingly uncomfortable being back in Greece, and so isolated here on Taygetos, at a former monastery. Kristian Koumantaros couldn't have found a more remote place to live if he'd tried.

"I would have thought your hair was all short and frizzy," he continued, "or up tight in a bun. You sound like a woman who'd wear her hair scraped back and tightly pinned up."

He was still trying to goad her, still trying to get a reaction. "I do like buns, yes. They're professional."

"And you're so *very* professional," he mocked.

She stiffened, her face paling. An icy lump hit her stomach.

Her former husband, another Greek playboy, had put her through two years of hell before they were finally legally separated, and it had taken her nearly five years to recover. One Greek playboy had already broken her heart. She refused to let another break her spirit.

Elizabeth squared her shoulders, lifted her head. "Since there's nothing else, Mr. Koumantaros, I'll say goodnight."

And before he could speak she'd exited the room and firmly shut the door behind her.

But Elizabeth's control snapped the moment she reached the hall. Swiftly, she put a hand out to brace herself against the wall.

She couldn't do this.

Couldn't stay here, live like this, be tormented like this.

She despised spoiled, pampered Greeks—particularly wealthy tycoons with far too much time on their hands.

After her divorce she'd vowed she'd never return to Greece, but here she was. Not just in Greece, but trapped on a mountain peak in a medieval monastery with Kristian Koumantaros, a man so rich, so powerful, he made Arab sheikhs look poor.

Elizabeth exhaled hard, breathing out in a desperate, painful rush.

She couldn't let tomorrow be a repeat of today, either. She was losing control of Koumantaros and the situation already.

This couldn't continue. Her patient didn't respect her, wasn't even listening to her, and he felt entirely too comfortable mocking her.

Elizabeth gave her head a slight dazed shake. How was this happening? She was supposed to be in charge.

Tomorrow, she told herself fiercely, returning to the bedroom the housekeeper had given her. Tomorrow she'd prove to him she was the one in charge, the one running the show.

She could do this. She had to.

The day had been warm, and although it was now night, her bedroom retained the heat. Like the other tower rooms, its plaster ceiling was high, at least ten or eleven feet, and decorated with elaborate painted friezes.

She crossed to open her windows and allow the evening breeze in. Her three arched windows overlooked the gardens, now bathed in moonlight, and then the mountain valley beyond.

It was beautiful here, uncommonly beautiful, with the ancient monastery tucked among rocks, cliffs and chestnut trees. But also incredibly dangerous. Kristian Koumantaros was a man used to dominating his world. She needed him to work with her, cooperate with her, or he could destroy her business and reputation completely.

At the antique marble bureau, Elizabeth twisted her long hair and then reached for one of her hair combs to fasten the knot on top of her head.

As she slid the comb in, she glanced up into the ornate silver filigree mirror over the bureau. Glimpsing her reflection—fair, light eyes, an oval face with a surprisingly strong chin—she grimaced. Back when she'd done more with herself, back when she'd had a luxurious lifestyle, she'd been a paler blonde, more like champagne, softer, prettier. But she'd given up the expensive highlights along with the New York and London stylists. She didn't own a single couture item anymore, nor any high-end real estate. The lifestyle she'd once known—taken for granted, assumed to be as much a part of her birthright as her name—was gone.

Over.

Forgotten.

But, turning back suddenly to the mirror, she saw the flicker in her eyes and knew she hadn't forgotten.

Medicine—nursing—offered her an escape, provided structure, a regimented routine and a satisfying amount of control. While medicine in and of itself wasn't safe, medicine coupled with business administration became something far more predictable. Far more manageable. Which was exactly what she prayed Kristian would be tomorrow.

* * *

The next morning Elizabeth woke early, ready to get to work, but even at seven the monastery-turned-villa was still dark except for a few lights in the kitchen.

Heartened that the villa was coming to life, Elizabeth dressed in a pale blue shirt and matching blue tailored skirt—her idea of a nursing uniform—before heading to find breakfast, which seemed to surprise the cook, throwing her into a state of anxiety and confusion.

Elizabeth managed to convince her that all she really needed was a cup of coffee and a bite to eat. The cook obliged with both, and over Greek coffee—undrinkable—and a *tiropita*, or cheese pie, Elizabeth visited with Pano.

She learned that Kristian usually slept in and then had coffee in his bed, before making his way to the library where he spent each day.

"What does he do all day?" she asked, breaking the pie into smaller bites. Pano hesitated, and then finally shrugged.

"He does nothing?" Elizabeth guessed.

Pano shifted his shoulders. "It is difficult for him."

"I understand in the beginning he did the physical therapy. But then something happened?"

"It was the eye surgery—the attempt to repair the retinas." Pano sighed heavily, and the same girl who'd served Elizabeth lunch yesterday came forward with fresh hot coffee. "He'd had some sight until then—not much, but enough that he could see light and shadows, shapes—but something went wrong in the repeated surgeries and he is now as you see him. Blind."

Elizabeth knew that losing the rest of his sight would have been a terrible blow. "I read in his chart that there is still a slight chance he could regain some sight with another treatment. It'd be minimal, I realize."

Elderly Pano shrugged.

"Why doesn't he do it?" she persisted.

"I think…" His wrinkled face wrinkled further. "He's afraid. It's his last hope."

Elizabeth said nothing, and Pano lifted his hands to try to make her understand.

"As long as he postpones the surgery, he can hope that one day he might see again. But once he has the surgery, and it doesn't work—" the old man snapped his fingers "—then there is nothing else for him to hope for."

And that Elizabeth actually understood.

But as the hours passed, and the morning turned to noon, Elizabeth grew increasingly less sympathetic.

What kind of life was this? To just sleep all day?

She peeked into his room just before twelve and he was still out, sprawled half-naked between white sheets, his dark hair tousled.

Elizabeth went in search of Pano once more, to enquire into Kristian's sleeping habits.

"Is it usual for Kirios Koumantaros to sleep this late?" she asked.

"It's not late. Not for him. He can sleep 'til one or two in the afternoon."

Unable to hide her incredulity, she demanded, "Did his other nurses allow this?"

Pano's bald head shone in the light as he bent over the big table and finished straightening the mail and papers piled there. "His other nurses couldn't control him. He is a man. He does as he wants to do."

"No. Not when his medical care costs thousands and thousands of pounds each week."

Mail sorted and newspapers straightened, Pano looked up at her. "You don't tell a grown man what to do."

She made a rough sound. "Yes, you do. If what he's doing is destructive."

Pano didn't answer, and after a glance at the tall library clock—it was now five minutes until one—she turned around and headed straight for Kristian's bedroom. What she found there, on his bedside table, explained his long, deep sleep.

He'd taken sleeping pills. She didn't know how many, and she didn't know when they'd been taken, but the bottle hadn't been there earlier in the evening when she'd checked on him.

She'd collected the bottles from the small table in the library and put them in her room, under lock and key, so for him to have had access to this bottle meant he had a secret stash of his own to medicate himself as he pleased.

But still, he couldn't get the prescriptions filled if Pano or another staff member weren't aiding him. Someone—and she suspected Pano again—was making it too easy for Kristian to be dependent.

Elizabeth spoke Kristian's name to wake him. No response. She said his name again. "Mr. Koumantaros, it's gone noon—time to wake up."

Nothing.

"Mr. Koumantaros." She stepped closer to the bed, stood over him and said, more loudly, "It's gone noon, Mr. Koumantaros. Time to get up. You can't sleep all day."

Kristian wasn't moving. He wasn't dead, either. She could see that much. He was breathing, and there was eye movement beneath his closed lids, but he certainly wasn't interested in waking up.

She cleared her throat and practically shouted, "Kristian Koumantaros—it's time to get up."

Kristian heard the woman. How could he not? She sounded as if she had a bullhorn. But he didn't want to wake.

He wanted to sleep.

He needed to keep sleeping, craved the deep dreamless sleep that would mercifully make all dark and quiet and peaceful.

But the voice didn't stop. It just grew louder. And louder.

Now there was a tug on the covers, and in the next moment they were stripped back, leaving him bare.

"Go away," he growled.

"It's gone noon, Mr. Koumantaros. Time to get up. Your first physical therapy session is in less than an hour."

And that was when he remembered. He wasn't dealing with just any old nurse, but nurse number seven. Elizabeth Hatchet. The latest nurse, an English nurse of all things, sent to make his life miserable.

He rolled over onto his stomach. "You're not allowed to wake me up."

"Yes, I am. It's gone noon and you can't sleep the day away."

"Why not? I was up most of the night."

"Your first physical therapy session begins soon."

"You're mad."

"Not mad, not even angry. Just ready to get you back into treatment, following a proper exercise program."

"No."

Elizabeth didn't bother to argue. There was no point. One way or another he would resume physical therapy. "Pano is on his way with breakfast. I told him you could eat in the dining room, like a civilized man, but he insisted he serve you in bed."

"Good man," Kristian said under his breath.

Elizabeth let this pass, too. "But this is your last morning being served in bed. You're neither an invalid nor a prince. You can eat at a table like the rest of us."

She rolled his wheelchair closer to the bed. "Your chair is here, in case you need it, and I'll be just a moment while I gather a few things." And with that she took the medicine bottle from the table and headed for the bathroom adjoining his bedroom. In the bathroom she quickly opened drawers and cupboard doors, before returning to his room with another two bottles in her hands.

"What are you doing?" Kristian asked, sitting up and listening to her open and close the drawers in his dresser.

"Looking for the rest of your secret stash."

"Secret stash of what?"

"You know perfectly well."

"If I knew, I wouldn't be asking."

She found another pill bottle at the back of his top drawer, right behind his belts. "Just how much stuff are you taking?"

"I take very little—"

"Then why do you have enough prescriptions and bottles to fill a pharmacy?"

It was his turn to fall silent, and she snorted as she finished checking his room. She found nothing else. Not in the armchair in the corner, or the drawer of the nightstand, nor between the mattresses of his bed. Good. Maybe she'd found the last of it. She certainly hoped so.

"Now what?" he asked, as Elizabeth scooped up the bottles and marched through the master bedroom's French doors outside to the pool.

"Just finishing the job," she said, leaving the French doors open and heading across the sunlit patio to the pool and fountain.

"Those are mine," he shouted furiously.

"Not anymore," she called back.

"I can't sleep without them—"

"You could if you got regular fresh air and exercise." Elizabeth was walking quickly, but not so fast that she couldn't hear Kristian make the awkward transfer from his bed into his wheelchair.

"Parakalo," he demanded. "Please. Wait a blasted moment."

She did. Only because it was the first time she'd heard him use the word *please*. As she paused, she heard Kristian hit the open door with a loud bang, before backing up and banging his way forward again, this time managing to get through. Just as clumsily he pushed across the pale stone deck, his chair tires humming on the deck.

"I waited," she said, walking again, "but I'm not giving them back. They're poison. They're absolutely toxic for you."

Kristian was gaining on her and, reaching the fountain, she popped the caps off the bottles and turned toward him.

His black hair was wild, and the scar on his cheek like face paint from an ancient tribe. He might very well have been one of the warring Greeks.

"Everything you put in your body," she said, trying to slow the racing of her heart, as well as the sickening feeling that she was once again losing control, "and everything you do to your body is my responsibility."

And with that she emptied the bottles into the fountain, the splash of pills loud enough to catch Kristian's attention.

"You did it," he said.

"I did," she agreed.

A line formed between his eyebrows and his cheekbones grew more pronounced. "I declare war, then," he said, and the edge of his mouth lifted, tilted in a dark smile. "War. War against your company, and war against you." His voice dropped, deepened. "I'm fairly certain that very soon, Ms. Hatchet, you will deeply regret ever coming here."

CHAPTER FOUR

ELIZABETH'S heart thumped hard. So hard she thought it would burst from her chest.

It was a threat. Not just a small threat, but one meant to send her to her knees.

For a moment she didn't know what to think, or do, and as her heart raced she felt overwhelmed by fear and dread. And then she found her backbone, and knew she couldn't let a man—much less a man like Kristian—intimidate her. She wasn't a timid little church mouse, nor a country bumpkin. She'd come from a family every bit as powerful as the Koumantaros family—not that she talked about her past, or wanted anyone to know about it.

"Am I supposed to be afraid, Mr. Koumantaros?" she asked, capping the bottles and dropping them in her skirt pocket. "You must realize you're not a very threatening adversary."

Drawing on her courage, she continued coolly, "You can hardly walk, and you can't see, and you depend on everyone else to take care of you. So, really, why should I be frightened? What's the worst you can do? Call me names?"

He leaned back in his wheelchair, his black hair a striking contrast to the pale stone wall behind him. "I don't know whether to admire your moxie or pity your naïveté."

The day hadn't started well, she thought with a deep sigh, and it was just getting worse. Everything with him was a battle. If he only focused half his considerable intelligence and energy on healing instead of baiting nurses he'd be walking by now, instead of sitting like a wounded caveman in his wheelchair.

"Pity?" she scoffed. "Don't pity me. You're the one that hasn't worked in a year. You're the one that needs your personal and business affairs managed by others."

"You take so many liberties."

"They're not liberties; they're truths. If you were half the man your friends say you are, you wouldn't still be hiding away and licking your wounds."

"Licking my wounds?" he repeated slowly.

"I know eight people died that day in France, and I know one of them was your brother. I know you tried to rescue him, and I know you were hurt going back for him. But you will not bring him back by killing yourself—" She broke off as he reached out and grasped her wrist with his hand.

Elizabeth tried to pull back, but he didn't let her go. "No personal contact, Mr. Koumantaros," she rebuked sternly, tugging at her hand. "There are strict guidelines for patient-nurse relationships."

He laughed as though she'd just told a joke. But he also swiftly released her. "I don't think your highly trained Calista got that memo."

She glanced down at her wrist, which suddenly burned, checking for marks. There were none. And yet her skin felt hot, tender, and she rubbed it nervously. "It's not a memo. It's an ethics standard. Every nurse knows there are lines that cannot be crossed. There are no gray areas on this one. It's very black and white."

"You might want to explain that one to Calista, because she *begged* me to make love to her. But then she also asked me for money—confusing for a patient, I can assure you."

The sun shone directly overhead, and the heat coming off the stone terrace was intense, and yet Elizabeth froze. "What do you mean, she asked you for money?"

"Surely the UK has its fair share of blackmail?"

"You're trying to shift responsibility and the blame," she said, glancing around quickly, suppressing panic. Panic because if Calista *had* attempted to blackmail Mr. Koumantaros, one of Greece's most illustrious sons…oh…bad. Very, very bad. It was so bad she couldn't even finish the thought.

Expression veiled, Kristian shrugged and rested his hands on the rims of his wheelchair tires. "But as you say, Cratchett, she was twenty-three—very young. Maybe she didn't realize it wasn't ethical to seduce a patient and then demand hush money." He paused. "Maybe she didn't realize that blackmailing me while being employed by First Class Rehab meant that First Class Rehab would be held liable."

Elizabeth's legs wobbled. She'd dealt with a lot of problems in the past year, had sorted out everything from poor budgeting to soaring travel costs, but she hadn't seen this one coming.

"And you *are* First Class Rehab, aren't you, Ms. Hatchet? It is your company?"

She couldn't speak. Her mouth dried. Her heart pounded. She was suddenly too afraid to make a sound.

"I did some research, Ms. Hatchet."

She very much wished there was a chair close by, something she could sit down on, but all the furniture had been exiled to one end of the terrace, to give Mr. Koumantaros more room to maneuver his wheelchair.

"Calista left here months ago," she whispered, plucking

back a bit of hair as the breeze kicked in. "Why didn't you come to me then? Why did you wait so long to tell me?"

His mouth slanted, his black lashes dropped, concealing his intensely blue eyes. "I decided I'd wait and see if the level of care improved. It did not—"

"You refused to cooperate!" she exclaimed, her voice rising.

"I'm thirty-six, a world traveler, head of an international corporation and not used to being dependent on anyone—much less young women. Furthermore, I'd just lost my brother, four of my best friends, a cousin, his girlfriend, and her best friend." His voice vibrated with fury. "It was a lot to deal with."

"Which is why we were trying to help you—"

"By sending me a twenty-three-year-old former exotic dancer?"

"She wasn't."

"She was. She had also posed topless in numerous magazines—not that I ever saw them; she just bragged about them, and about how men loved her breasts. They were natural, you see."

Elizabeth was shaking. This was bad—very bad—and getting worse. "Mr. Koumantaros—" she pleaded.

But he didn't stop. "You say you personally hire and train every nurse? You say you do background reports and conduct all the interviews?"

"In the beginning, yes, I did it all. And I still interview all of the UK applicants."

"But *you* don't personally screen every candidate? You don't do the background checks yourself anymore, either. Do you?"

The tension whipped through her, tightening every muscle and nerve. "No."

He paused, as though considering her. "Your agency literature says you do."

Sickened, Elizabeth bit her lip, feeling trapped, cornered. She'd never worked harder than she had in the past year. She'd never accomplished so much, or fought so many battles, either. "We've grown a great deal in the past year. Doubled in size. I've been stretched—"

"Now listen to who has all the excuses."

Blood surged to her cheeks, making her face unbearably warm. She supposed she deserved that. "I've offices in seven cities, including Athens, and I employ hundreds of women throughout Europe. I'd vouch for nearly every one of them."

"Nearly?" he mocked. "So much for First Class Rehab's guarantee of first-class care and service."

Elizabeth didn't know which way to turn. "I'd be happy to rewrite our company mission statement."

"I'm sure you will be." His mouth curved slowly. "Once you've finished providing me with the quality care I so desperately need." His smile stretched. "As well as deserve."

She crossed her arms over her chest, shaken and more than a little afraid. "Does that mean you'll be working with me this afternoon on your physical therapy?" she asked, finding it so hard to ask the question that her voice was but a whisper.

"No, it means you will be working with me." He began rolling forward, slowly pushing himself back to the tower rooms. "I imagine it's one now, which means lunch will be served in an hour. I'll meet you for lunch, and we can discuss my thoughts on my therapy then."

Elizabeth spent the next hour in a state of nervous shock. She couldn't absorb anything from the conversation she'd had with Kristian on the patio. Couldn't believe everything she'd thought, everything she knew, was just possibly wrong.

She'd flown Calista into London for her final interview. It

had been an all-expenses paid trip, too, and Calista had impressed Elizabeth immediately as a warm, energetic, dedicated nurse. A true professional. There was no way she could be, or ever have been, an exotic dancer. Nor a topless model. Impossible.

Furthermore, Calista wouldn't *dream* of seducing a man like Kristian Koumantaros. She was a good Greek girl, a young woman raised in Piraeus, the port of Athens, with her grandmother and a spinster great-aunt. Calista had solid family values.

And not much money.

Elizabeth closed her eyes, shook her head once, not wanting to believe the worst.

Then don't, she told herself, opening her eyes and heading for her room, to splash cold water on her face. Don't believe the worst. Look for the best in people. Always.

And yet as she walked through the cool arched passages of the tower to her own room a little voice whispered, *Isn't that why you married a man like Nico? Because you only wanted to believe the best in him?*

Forty-five minutes later, Elizabeth returned downstairs, walking outside to the terrace where she'd had a late lunch yesterday. She discovered Kristian was already there, enjoying his coffee.

Elizabeth, remembering her own morning coffee, grimaced inwardly. She'd always thought that Greek coffee—or what was really Turkish coffee—tasted like sludge. Nico had loved the stuff, and had made fun of her preference for *café au lait* and cappuccino, but she'd grown up with a coffee house on every corner in New York, and a latte or a mocha was infinitely preferable to thick black mud.

At her footsteps Kristian lifted his head and looked up in her direction. Her breath caught in her throat.

Kristian had shaved. His thick black hair had been trimmed and combed, and as he turned his attention on her the blue of his eyes was shocking. Intense. Maybe even more intense without sight, as he was forced to focus, to really listen.

His blue eyes were such a sharp contrast to his black hair and hard, masculine features that she felt an odd shiver race through her—a shiver of awareness, appreciation—and it bewildered her, just as nearly everything about this man threw her off balance. For a moment she felt what Calista must have felt, confronted by a man like this.

"Hello." Elizabeth sat down, suddenly shy. "You look nice," she added, her voice coming out strangely husky.

"A good shave goes a long way."

It wasn't just the shave, she thought, lifting her napkin from the table and spreading it across her lap. It was the alert expression on Kristian's face, the sense that he was there, mentally, physically, clearly paying attention.

"I am very sorry about the communication problems," she said, desperately wanting to start over, get things off on a better foot. "I understand you are very frustrated, and I want you to know I am eager to make everything better—"

"I know," he interrupted quietly.

"You do?"

"You're afraid I'll destroy your company." One black eyebrow quirked. "And it would be easy to do, too. Within a month you'd be gone."

There wasn't a cloud in the sky, and yet the day suddenly grew darker, as though the sun itself had dimmed. "Mr. Koumantaros—"

"Seeing as we're going to be working so closely together, isn't it time we were on a first-name basis?" he suggested.

She eyed him warily. He was reminding her of a wild

animal at the moment—dangerous and unpredictable. "That might be difficult."

"And why is that?"

She wondered if she should be honest, wondered if now was the time to flatter him, win him over with insincere compliments, and then decided against it. She'd always been truthful, and she'd remain so now. "The name Kristian doesn't suit you at all. It implies Christ-like, and you're far from that."

She had expected him to respond with anger. Instead he smiled faintly, the top of his finger tapping against the rim of his cup. "My mother once said she'd given us the wrong names. My older brother Andreas should have had my name, and she felt I would have been better with his. Andreas—or Andrew—in Greek means—"

"Strong," she finished for him. "Manly. Courageous."

Kristian's head lifted as though he could see her. She knew he could not, and she felt a prick of pain for him. Vision was so important. She relied on her eyes for everything.

"I've noticed you're fluent in Greek," he said thoughtfully. "That's unusual, considering your background."

He didn't know her background. He didn't know anything about her. But now wasn't the time to be correcting him. In an effort to make peace, she was willing to be conciliatory. "So, you are the strong one and your brother was the saint?"

Kristian shrugged. "He's dead, and I'm alive."

And, even though she wanted peace, she couldn't help thinking that Kristian really was no saint. He'd been a thorn in her side from the beginning, and she was anxious to be rid of him. "You said earlier that you were willing to start your therapy, but you want to be in charge of your rehabilitation program?"

He nodded. "That's right. You are here to help me accomplish my goals."

"Great. I'm anxious to help you meet your goals." She crossed her legs and settled her hands in her lap. "So, what do you want me to do?"

"Whatever it is I need done."

Elizabeth's mouth opened, then closed. "That's rather vague," she said, when she finally found her voice.

"Oh, don't worry. It won't be vague. I'll be completely in control. I'll tell you what time we start our day, what time we finish, and what we do in between."

"What about the actual exercises? The stretching, the strengthening—"

"I'll take care of that."

He would devise his own course of treatment? He would manage his rehabilitation program?

Her head spun. She couldn't think her way clear. This was all too ridiculous. But then finally, fortunately, logic returned. "Mr. Koumantaros, you might be an excellent executive, and able to make millions of dollars, but that doesn't mean you know the basics of physical therapy—"

"Nurse Hatchet, I haven't walked because I haven't wanted to walk. It's as simple as that."

"Is it?"

"Yes."

My God, he was arrogant—and overly confident. "And you want to walk now?"

"Yes."

Weakly she leaned back in her chair and stared at him. Kristian was changing before her eyes. Metamorphosing.

Pano and the housekeeper appeared with their lunch, but Kristian paid them no heed. "You were the one who told me I need to move forward, Cratchett, and you're absolutely right. It's time I moved forward and got back on my feet."

She watched the myriad of small plates set before them. *Mezedhes*—lots of delicious dips, ranging from eggplant purée to cucumber, yoghurt and garlic, cheese. There were also plates of steaming *keftedhes, dolmadhes, tsiros.* And it all smelled amazing. Elizabeth might not love Greek coffee, but she loved Greek food. Only right now it would be impossible to eat a bite of anything.

"And when do you intend to start your…program?" she asked.

"Today. Immediately after lunch." He sat still while Pano moved the plates around for him, and quietly explained where the plates were and what each dish was.

When Pano and the housekeeper had left, Kristian continued. "I want to be walking soon. I need to be walking this time next week if I hope to travel to Athens in a month's time."

"Walking next *week?*" she choked, unable to take it all in. She couldn't believe the change in him. Couldn't believe the swift turn of events, either. From waking him, to the pills being dumped into the fountain, to the revelation about Calista—everything was different.

Everything, she repeated silently, but especially him. And just looking at him from across the table she saw he seemed so much bigger. Taller. More imposing.

"A week," he insisted.

"Kristian, it's good to have goals. But please be realistic. It's highly unlikely you'll be able to walk unaided in the next couple of weeks, but with hard work you might manage short distances with your walker—"

"If I go to Athens there can be no walker."

"But—"

"It's a matter of culture and respect, Ms. Hatchet. You're not Greek; you don't understand—"

"I *do* understand. That's why I'm here. But give yourself time to meet your goals. Two or three months is far more realistic."

With a rough push of his wheelchair, he rolled back a short distance from the table. "Enough!"

Slowly he placed one foot on the ground, and then the other, and then, leaning forward, put his hands on the table. For a moment it seemed as though nothing was happening, and then, little by little, he began to push up, utilizing his triceps, biceps and shoulders to give himself leverage.

His face paled and perspiration beaded his brow. Thick jet-black hair fell forward as, jaw set, he continued to press up until he was fully upright.

As soon as he was straight he threw his head back in an almost primal act of conquest. *"There."* The word rumbled from him.

He'd proved her wrong.

It had cost him to stand unassisted, too. She could see from his pallor and the lines etched at his mouth that he was hurting, but he didn't utter a word of complaint.

She couldn't help looking at him with fresh respect. What he had done had not been easy. It had taken him long, grueling minutes to concentrate, to work muscles that hadn't been utilized in far too long. But he had succeeded. He'd stood by himself.

And he'd done it as an act of protest and defiance.

He'd done it as something to prove.

"That's a start," she said crisply, hiding her awe. He wasn't just any man. He was a force to be reckoned with. "It's impressive. But you know it's just going to get harder from here."

Kristian shifted his weight, steadied himself, and removed one hand from the table so that he already stood taller.

Silent emotion flickered across his beautiful scarred face. "Good," he said. "I'm ready."

Reaching back for his wheelchair, he nearly stumbled, and Elizabeth jumped to her feet even as Pano rushed forward from the shadows.

Kristian angrily waved both off. *"Ohi!"* he snapped, strain evident in the deep lines shaping his mouth. "No."

"Kyrios," Pano pleaded, pained to see Kristian struggle so.

But Kristian rattled off a rebuke in furious Greek. "I can do it," he insisted, after taking a breath. "I *must* do it."

Pano reluctantly dropped back, and Elizabeth slowly sat down again, torn between admiration and exasperation. While she admired the fact that Kristian would not allow anyone to help him be reseated, she also knew that if he went at his entire therapy like this he'd soon be exhausted, frustrated, and possibly injured worse.

He needed to build his strength gradually, with a systematic and scientific approach.

But Kristian had a different plan—which he outlined after lunch.

Standing—walking—was merely an issue of mind over matter, he said, and her job wasn't to provide obstacles, tell him no, or even offer advice. Her job was to be there when he wanted something, and that was it.

"I'm a handmaid?" she asked, trying to hide her indignation. After four years earning a nursing degree, and then another two years earning a Masters in Business Administration? "You could hire anyone to come and play handmaid. I'm a little over-qualified and rather expensive—"

"I know," he said grimly. "Your agency charged an exorbitant amount for my care—little good did it do me."

"You chose not to improve."

"Your agency's methods were useless."

"I protest."

"You may protest all you like, but it doesn't change the facts. Under your agency's care, not only did I fail to recover, but I was harassed as well as blackmailed. The bottom line, Kyria Hatchet, is that not only did you milk the system—and me—for hundreds and thousands of euros, but you also dared to show up here, uninvited, unwanted, and force yourself on me."

Sick at heart, she rose. "I'll leave, then. Let's just forget this—pretend it never happened—"

"What about the doctors, Nurse? What about those specialists who insisted you come here or I go to their facility in Athens? Was that true, or another of your lies?"

"Lies?"

"I know why you're here—"

"To get you better!"

"You have exactly ten seconds to give me the full name and contact number of the person now responsible for paying my medical bills or I shall begin dismantling your company within the hour. All it will take is one phone call to my office in Athens and your life as you know it will be forever changed."

"Kristian—"

"Nine seconds."

"Kris—"

"Eight."

"I promised—"

"Seven."

"A deal is—"

"Six."

Livid tears scalded her eyes. "It's because she cares. It's because she loves you—"

"Four."

"She wants you back. Home. Close to her."

"Two."

Elizabeth balled her hands into fists. *"Please."*

"One."

"Cosima." She pressed one fist to her chest, to slow the panicked beating of her heart. "Cosima hired me. She's desperate. She just wants you home."

CHAPTER FIVE

COSIMA?

Kristian's jaw hardened and his voice turned flinty. How could Cosima possibly pay for his care? She might be Andreas's former fiancée and Athens's most popular socialite, but she had more financial problems than anyone he knew.

"Cosima hired you?" he repeated, thinking maybe he'd heard wrong. "She was the one that contacted you in London?"

"Yes. But I promised her—*promised*—I wouldn't tell you."

"Why?"

"She said you'd be very upset if you knew, she said you were so proud—" Elizabeth broke off, the threat of tears evident in her voice. "She said she had to do something to show you how much she believed in you."

Cosima believed in him?

Kristian silently, mockingly, repeated Elizabeth's words. Or maybe it was that Cosima felt indebted to him. Maybe she felt as guilt-ridden as he did. Because, after all, she lived and Andreas had died, and it was Kristian who'd made the decision. It was Kristian who'd played God that day.

No wonder he had nightmares. No wonder he had nightmares during the day.

He couldn't accept the decision he'd made. Nor could he accept that it was a decision that couldn't be changed.

Kristian, wealthy and powerful beyond measure, couldn't buy or secure the one thing he wanted most: his brother's life.

But Elizabeth knew nothing of Kristian's loathing, and anger, and pressed on. "Now that you know," she continued, "the contract isn't valid. I can't remain—"

"Of course you can," he interrupted shortly. "She doesn't have to know that I know. There's no point in wrecking her little plan."

His words were greeted by silence, and for a moment he thought maybe Elizabeth had left, going God knew where, but then he heard the faintest shuffle, and an even softer sigh.

"She just wants what is best for you," Elizabeth said wearily. "Please don't be angry with her. She seems like such a kind person."

It was in that moment that Kristian learned something very important about Elizabeth Hatchet.

Elizabeth Hatchet might have honest intentions, but she was a lousy judge of character.

It was on the tip of his tongue to ask if Elizabeth was aware that Cosima and Calista had gone to school together. To ask her if she knew that both women had shared a flat for more than a year, and had gone into modeling together, too.

He could tell her that Calista and Cosima had been the best of friends until their lives had gone in very different directions.

Cosima had met Andreas Koumantaros and become girlfriend and then fiancée to one of Greece's most wealthy men.

Calista, unable to find a rich enough boyfriend, or enough modeling jobs to pay her rent, had turned to exotic dancing and questionable modeling gigs.

The two seemed to have had nothing more in common after

a couple years. Cosima had traveled the world as the pampered bride-to-be, and Calista had struggled to make ends meet.

And then tragedy had struck and evened the score.

Andreas had died in the avalanche, Cosima had survived but lost her lifestyle, and Calista, who had still been struggling along, had thought she'd found a sugar-daddy of her own.

Albeit a handicapped one.

The corner of his mouth curved crookedly, the tilt of his lips hiding the depth of his anger as well as his derision. Calista hadn't been the first to imagine he'd be an easy conquest. A dozen women from all over Europe had flocked to his side during his hospital stay. They'd brought flowers, gifts, seductive promises. *I love you. I'll be here for you. I'll never leave you.*

It would have been one thing if any of them had genuinely cared for him. Instead they'd all been opportunists, thinking a life with an invalid wouldn't be so bad if the invalid was a Greek tycoon.

Again Kristian felt the whip of anger. Did women think that just because he couldn't see he'd lost his mind?

That his inability to travel unaided across the room meant he'd enjoy the company of a shallow, self-absorbed, materialistic woman? He hadn't enjoyed shallow and self-absorbed women before. Why would he now?

"You've met Cosima, then," he said flatly.

"We've only spoken on the phone, but her concern—and she *is* concerned—touched me," Elizabeth added anxiously, trying to fill the silence. "She obviously has a good heart, and it wouldn't be fair to punish her for trying to help you."

Kristian ran his hand over his jaw. "No, you're right. And you said, she seems most anxious to see me on my feet."

"Yes. Yes—and she's just so worried about you. She

was in tears on the phone. I think she's afraid you're shutting her out—"

"Really?" This did intrigue him. Was Cosima possibly imagining some kind of future for the two of them? The idea was as grotesque as it was laughable.

"She said you've become too reclusive here."

"This is my home."

"But she's concerned you're overly depressed and far too despondent."

"Were those her actual words?" he asked, struggling to keep the sarcasm from his voice.

"Yes, as a matter of fact. I have it in my notes, if you want to see—"

"No. I believe you." His brows flattened, his curiosity colored by disbelief. Cosima wasn't sentimental. She wasn't particularly emotional or sensitive, either. So why would she be so anxious to have him return to Athens? "And so," he added, wanting to hear more about Cosima's concern, "you were sent here to rescue me."

"Not rescue, just motivate you. Get you on your feet."

"And look!" he said grandly, gesturing with his hands. "Today I stood. Tomorrow I climb Mount Everest."

"Not Everest," Elizabeth corrected, sounding genuinely bemused. "Just walk in time for your wedding."

Wedding?

Wedding?

Kristian had heard it all now. He didn't know whether to roar with amusement or anguish. His wedding. To Cosima, his late brother's lover, he presumed. My God, this was like an ancient Greek comedy—a bold work conceived of by Aristophanes. One full of bawdy mirth but founded on tragedy.

And as he sat there, trying to take it all in, Cosima and Calista's scheming reminded him of the two Greek sisters: Penia, goddess of poverty, and Amakhania, goddess of helplessness. Goddesses known for tormenting with their evil and greed.

But now that he knew, he wouldn't be tormented any longer.

No, he'd write a little Greek play of his own. And if all went well his good Nurse Cratchett could even help him by playing a leading role.

"Let's not tell her I know," Kristian said. "Let's work hard, and we'll surprise her with my progress."

"So where do we start?" Elizabeth asked. "What do we do first?"

He nearly smiled at her enthusiasm. She sounded so pleased with him already. "*I've* already hired a physical therapist from Sparta," he answered, making it clear that this was not a joint decision, but his and his alone. "The therapist arrives tomorrow."

"And until then?"

"I'll probably relax, nap. Swim."

"Swim?" she asked. "You're swimming?"

Her surprise made his lip curl. She really thought he was in dreadful shape, didn't she? "I have been for the past two weeks."

"Ever since your last nurse left?" she said quietly.

He didn't answer. He didn't need to.

"Maybe you could show me the pool?" she asked.

For a moment he almost felt sorry for her. She was trying so hard to do what she thought was the right thing, but her idea of right wasn't necessarily what he wanted or needed. "Of course. If you'll come with me."

Together they traveled across the stone courtyard with its trellis-covered patio, where they'd just enjoyed lunch, with

Kristian pushing his own wheelchair and Elizabeth walking next to him.

They headed toward the fountain and then passed it, moving from the stone patio to the garden, with its gravel path.

"The gardens are beautiful," Elizabeth said, walking slowly enough for Kristian to push his chair at a comfortable pace.

His tires sank into the gravel, and he wrestled a moment with his chair until he found traction again and pushed faster, to keep from sinking back into the crushed stones. "You'd do better with a stone path here, wouldn't you?" she asked, glancing down at his arms, impressed by his strength.

Warm color darkened his cheekbones. "It was suggested months ago that I change it, but I knew I wouldn't be in a wheelchair forever so I left it."

"So you planned on getting out of your wheelchair?"

His head lifted, and he shot her a look as though he could see, his brow furrowing, lines deepening between his eyes. He resented her question, and his resentment brought home yet again just who he was, and what he'd accomplished in his lifetime.

Watching him struggle through the gravel, it crossed her mind that maybe he hadn't remained in the wheelchair because he was lazy, but because without sight he felt exposed. Maybe for him the wheelchair wasn't transportation so much as a suit of armor, a form of protection.

"Are we almost to the hedge?" he asked, pausing a moment to try and get his bearings.

"Yes, it's just in front of us."

"The pool, then, is to the left."

Elizabeth turned toward her left and was momentarily dazzled by the sun's reflection off brilliant blue water. The long lap pool sparkled in its emerald-green setting, making it appear even more jewel-like than it already was.

"It's a new pool?" she guessed, from the young landscaping and the gorgeous artisan tilework.

"I wish I could say it was my only extravagance, but I've been renovating the monastery for nearly a decade now. It's been a labor of love."

They'd reached a low stone wall that bordered the pool, and Elizabeth moved forward to open the pretty gate. "But why Taygetos? Why a ruined monastery? You don't have family from here, do you?"

"No, but I love the mountains—this is where I feel at home," he said, lifting a hand to his face as if to block the sun. "My mother was French, raised in a small town at the base of the Alps. I've grown up hiking, skiing, rock-climbing. These are the things my father taught us to do, things my mother enjoyed, and it just feels right living here."

Elizabeth saw how he kept trying to shield his eyes with his hand. "Is the sun bothering you?"

"I usually wear bandages, or dark glasses."

"You've that much light sensitivity?"

"It's painful," he admitted.

She didn't want him in pain, but the tenderness and sensitivity gave her hope that maybe, one day, he might get at least a little of his vision back. "Shall I call Pano to get your glasses?"

"It's not necessary. We won't be here long."

"But it's lovely out," she said wistfully, gazing around the pool area and admiring the tiny purplish campanula flowers that were growing up and over the stone walls. The tiny violet-hued blossoms were such a pretty contrast to the rugged rock. "Let me get them. That way you can relax a little, be more comfortable."

"No, just find me a little shade—or perhaps position me away from the sun."

"There's some shade on the other side of the pool, near the rock wall." She hesitated. "Shall I push you?"

"I can do it myself."

But somehow in the struggle, as Elizabeth pushed forward and Kristian grappled for control, the front castors of his chair ran off the stone edge and over the side, and once the front casters went forward, the rest of the chair followed.

He hit the pool with a big splash.

It all happened in slow motion.

Just before he hit the water Elizabeth could see herself grabbing at his chair, hanging tight to the handles and trying to pull him back, but she was unable to get enough leverage to stop the momentum. In the end she let go, knowing she couldn't stop him and afraid she'd fall on him and hurt him worse.

Heart pounding, Elizabeth dropped to her knees, horrified that her patient and his wheelchair had just tumbled in.

How could she have let this happen? How could she have been so reckless?

Elizabeth was close to jumping in when Kristian surfaced. His chair, though, was another matter. While Kristian was swimming toward the side of the pool, his chair was slowly, steadily, sinking to the bottom.

"Kristian—I'm sorry, I'm sorry," she apologized repeatedly as she knelt on the pool deck. She'd never felt less professional in her entire life. An accident like this was pure carelessness. He knew it, and so did she.

"I cut the corner too close. I should have been paying closer attention. I'm so sorry."

He swam toward her.

Leaning forward, she extended her hand as far as it would

go. "You're almost at the wall. My hand's right in front of it. You've almost got it," she encouraged as he reached for her.

His fingers curled around hers. Relief surged through her. He was fine. "I've got you," she said.

"Are you sure?" he asked, hand tightening on hers. "Or do I have you?"

And, with a hard tug, he pulled her off her knees and into the pool.

Elizabeth landed hard on her stomach, splashing water wildly.

He'd pulled her in. Deliberately. She couldn't believe it. So much for poor, helpless Kristian Koumantaros.

He was far from helpless. And he'd fooled her three times now.

Spluttering to the surface, she looked around for Kristian and spotted him leaning casually against the wall.

"That was mean," she said, swimming toward him, her wet clothes hampering her movements.

He laughed softly and ran a hand through his hair, pushing the inky black strands back from his face. "I thought you'd find it refreshing."

She squeezed water from her own hair. "I didn't want you to fall in. I'd never want that to happen."

"Your concern for my wellbeing is most touching. You know, Cratchett, I was worried you might be like my other nurses, but I have to tell you, you're worse."

She swallowed hard. She deserved that. "I'm sorry," she said, knowing a responsible nurse would never have permitted such a thing to happen. Indeed, if any of her nurses had allowed a patient in their care to fall into a pool she'd have fired the nurse on the spot. "It's been a while since I actually did any in-home care. As you know, I'm the head administrator for the company now."

"Skills a little rusty?" he said.

"Mmmm." Using the ladder, she climbed out and sat down on the deck, to pluck at her shirt and tug her soggy shoes off.

"So why are *you* here and not another nurse?"

Wringing water from her skirt, she sighed. Defeated. "The agency's close to bankruptcy. I couldn't afford to send another nurse. It was me or nothing."

"But my insurance has paid you, and I've paid you."

Elizabeth watched the water trickle from her skirt to the stone pavers. "There were expenses not covered, and those costs were difficult to manage, and eventually they ate into the profits until we were barely breaking even." She didn't bother to tell him that Calista had needed counseling and compensation after leaving Kristian's employment. And covering Calista's bills had cost her dearly, too.

"I think I better get your chair," she said, not wanting to think about things she found very difficult to control.

"I do need it," he agreed. "Are you a strong swimmer?"

"I can swim."

"You're not inspiring much confidence, Cratchett."

She smiled despite herself. "It'll be okay." And it would be. She wasn't going to panic about holding her breath or swimming deep under water. She'd just go down and grab the chair, and haul it back up.

He sighed, pushed back wet hair from his face. "You're scared."

"No."

"You're not a very good swimmer."

She made a little exasperated sound. "I can swim laps. Pretty well. It's just in deep water I get…nervous."

"Claustrophobic?"

"Oh, it's silly, but—" She broke off, not wanting to tell him.

She didn't need him making fun of her. It was a genuine fear, and there wasn't a lot she could do about it.

"But what?"

"I had an accident when I was little." He said nothing, and she knew he was still waiting for the details. "I was playing a diving game with a girl I'd met. We'd toss coins and then go pick them up. Well, in this hotel pool there was a huge drain at the bottom, and somehow—" She broke off, feeling a little sick from the retelling. "There was a lot of suction, and somehow the strings on my swimsuit got tangled, stuck. I couldn't get them out and couldn't get my suit off."

Kristian didn't speak, and Elizabeth tried to smile. "They got me out, of course. Obviously. Here I am. But…" She felt a painful flutter inside, a memory of panic and what it had been like. Her shoulders lifted, fell. "I was scared."

"How old were you?"

"Six."

"You must have been a good swimmer to be playing diving games in the deep end at six."

She laughed a little. "I think as a little girl I was a bit on the wild side. My nanny—" She broke off, rephrased. "Anyway, after that I didn't want to swim anymore. Especially not in big pools. And since then I've pretty much stuck to the shallow end. Kind of boring, but safe."

Elizabeth could feel Kristian's scrutiny even though he couldn't see her. He was trying to understand her, to reconcile what he'd thought he knew with this.

"I'll make you a deal," he said at last.

Her eyes narrowed. So far his deals had been terrible. "What kind of deal?"

"I'll go get my own chair if you don't look while I strip. I can't dive down in my clothes."

Elizabeth pulled her knees up to her chest and tried not to laugh. "You're afraid I'll see you naked?"

"I'm trying to protect you. You're a nurse without a lot of field experience lately. I'm afraid my…nudity…might overwhelm you."

She grinned against her wet kneecap. "Fine."

One black eyebrow arched. "Fine, what? Fine, you'll look at me? Or fine, you'll politely avert your gaze?"

"Fine. I'll politely avert my gaze."

"Endaxi," he said, still in the pool. "Okay." And then he began peeling his clothes off one by one.

And although Elizabeth had made a promise not to look, the sound of wet cotton inching its way off wet skin was too tempting.

She did watch, and as the clothes came off she discovered he had a rather amazing body, despite the accident and horrific injuries. His torso was still powerful, thick with honed muscle, while from her vantage point on the deck his legs looked long and well shaped.

Clothes gone, he disappeared beneath the surface, swimming toward the bottom with strong, powerful strokes. Even though he couldn't see, he was heading in the right direction. It took him a moment to find the chair's exact location, but once he found it he took hold of the back and immediately began to swim up with it.

Incredible.

As Kristian surfaced with the chair, Pano and one of the housemaids came running through the small wrought-iron gate with a huge stack of towels.

"Kyrios," Pano called, "are you all right?"

"I'm fine." Kristian answered, dragging the chair to the side of the pool.

Pano was there to take the chair. He tipped it sideways and water streamed from the spokes and castors. He tipped it the other way and more water spurted from open screwholes, and then he passed the chair to the maid, who began vigorously toweling the wheelchair dry.

In the meantime Kristian placed his hands on the stone deck and hauled himself up and out, using only his shoulders, biceps and triceps. He was far stronger than he let on, and far more capable of taking care of himself than she'd thought.

He didn't need anyone pushing him.

He probably didn't need anyone taking care of him.

If everyone just stepped back and left him alone, she suspected that soon he'd manage just fine.

And, speaking of fine, Elizabeth couldn't tear her eyes from Kristian's broad muscular back, lean waist, and tight hard buttocks as he shifted his weight around. His body was almost perfectly proportioned, every muscle shaped and honed. He didn't look ill, or like a patient. He looked like a man, an incredibly physical, virile man.

Once his thighs had cleared the water he did a quick turn and sat down. Pano swiftly draped a towel over Kristian's shoulders and threw another one over his lap, but not before Elizabeth had seen as much of Kristian's front as she had seen of his back.

And his front was even more impressive. His shoulders broad and thick, his chest shaped into two hard planes of muscle, his belly flat, lean, and his…

His…

She shouldn't be staring at his lap, it was completely unprofessional, but he was very, very big there, too.

She felt blood surge to her cheeks, and she battled shyness, shame and interest.

His body was so beautiful, and his size, that symbol of masculinity—wow. Ridiculously impressive. And Elizabeth wasn't easily impressed.

No wonder Kristian was so comfortable naked. Even after a year plus in a wheelchair he was still every inch a man.

"I thought we had a deal," Kristian murmured, dragging the towel over his head and then his chest.

"We did. We do." Flushing crimson, Elizabeth jumped to her feet and twisted her damp skirt yet again. "Maybe I should go get some dry clothes."

"A good idea," Kristian said, leaning back on his hands, face lifted. He was smiling a little, a smile that indicated he knew she'd been looking at him, knew she'd been fascinated by his anatomy. "I wouldn't want you to catch a chill."

"No."

His lips curled, and the sunlight played over the carved planes of his face, lingering on the jagged scar, and she felt her heart leap at the savage violence done to his Greek beauty. "I'll see you at dinner, then."

See her at dinner.

He couldn't see her, of course, but he'd meet her, and her heart did another peculiar flutter. "Dinner tonight?"

"I thought I was to eat all my meals with you," he answered lazily. "Something about you needing to socialize me. Make me civil again."

Her heart was drumming a mile a minute. "Right." She forced a tight, pained smile. "I'll look forward to that…then."

Elizabeth turned so quickly that she stubbed her toe. With a hop and a whimper she set off at a run for the sanctuary of her room, lecturing herself the entire way. *Do not get personally involved, do not get personally involved, no matter what you do, do not get personally involved.*

But as she reached her tower bedroom and began to strip her wet clothes off she almost cried with vexation.

She already was involved.

CHAPTER SIX

OUTSIDE in the garden, as Kristian struggled to make his way back to the villa, water dripped from the chair and his cushion sagged, waterlogged.

Thank God he was almost done with this wheelchair.

Falling into the pool today had been infuriating and insightful. He hated how helpless he'd felt as he went blindly tumbling in. He'd hated the shock and surprise as he'd thrashed in his clothes in the water. But at the same time his unexpected fall had had unexpected results.

For one, Elizabeth had dropped some of her brittle guard, and he'd discovered she was far less icy then he'd thought. She was in many ways quite gentle, and her fear about the deep end had struck home with him. As a boy he'd been thrown from a horse, and he hadn't ridden again for years.

Getting back into the wet wheelchair had been another lesson. As he'd been transferred in, he'd realized the chair had served its purpose. He didn't want it anymore—didn't want to be confined or contained. He craved freedom, and knew that for the first time since his accident he was truly ready for whatever therapy was required to allow him to walk and run again.

Water still dripping, he cautiously rolled his way from grass to patio, and from patio toward the wing where his room was.

But as he rolled down the loggia he couldn't seem to find his bedroom door. He began to second-guess himself, and soon thought he'd gone the wrong way.

Pano, who'd been following several paces behind, couldn't keep silent any longer. "*Kyrie,* your room is just here." And, without waiting for Kristian to find it himself, the butler steered the wheelchair around the corner and over the door's threshold.

Kristian felt a tinge of annoyance at the help. He'd wanted to do it alone, felt an increasing need to do more for himself, but Pano, a good loyal employee of the past fifteen years, couldn't bear for Kristian to struggle.

"How did you end up in the pool?" Pano asked, closing the outside door.

Kristian shrugged and tugged the wet towel from around his shoulders. "Ms. Hatchet was pushing me toward the shade and misjudged the distance to the pool's edge."

"*Despinis* pushed you into the pool?" Pano cried, horrified.

"It was an accident."

"How could she push you into the pool?"

"It was a tight corner."

"How can that happen? How is that proper?" The butler muttered to himself as he opened and closed drawers, retrieving dry clothes for his master. "I knew she wasn't a proper nurse—knew she couldn't do the job. I *knew* it."

Kristian checked his smile. Pano was a traditional Greek, from the old school of hearth and home. "And how is she not a proper nurse?"

"If you could see—"

"But I can't. So you must tell me."

"First, she doesn't act like one, and second, she doesn't *look* like one."

"Why not? Is she too old, too heavy, what?"

"Ohi," Pano groaned. "No. She's not too old, or too fat, or anything like that. It's the opposite. She's too small. She's delicate. Like a little bird in a tiny cage. And if you want a little blonde bird for a nurse, fine. But if you need a big, sturdy woman to lift and carry…" Pano sighed, shrugging expressively. "Then Despinis Elizabeth is not for you."

So she was blonde, Kristian thought after Pano had left him alone to dress.

And Elizabeth Hatchet was neither old nor unattractive. Rather she was fine-boned, slender, a lady.

Kristian tried to picture her, this ladylike nurse of his, who hadn't actually nursed in years, who proclaimed Cosima kind, and as a child had stayed at hotels with a nanny to look after her.

But it was impossible to visualize her. He'd dated plenty of fair English and American girls, Scandinavians and Dutch, but he would have wagered a thousand euros Elizabeth was brunette.

But wasn't that like her? So full of surprises. For example her voice—melodic, like that of a violin—and her fragrance—not floral, not exotic spice, but fresh, clean, grass or melon. And then last night, when she'd leaned close to his bed to adjust his pillows, he'd been surprised she wore her hair down. Something about her brisk manner had made him assume she was the classic all-business, no-nonsense executive.

Apparently he was wrong.

Apparently his Cratchett was blonde, slender, delicate, *pretty.* Not even close to a battleaxe.

In trying to form a new impression of her, he wondered at her age, and her height, as well as the shade of her hair. Was she a pale, silvery blonde? Or a golden blonde with streaks of warm amber and honey?

But it wasn't just her age or appearance that intrigued him. It was her story, too, of a six-year-old who'd once been a daring swimmer now afraid to leave the shallow end, as well as the haunting image of a child trapped, swimsuit ties tangled, in that pool's powerful drain.

In her bedroom, after several lovely long hours devoted to nothing but reading and taking a delicious and much needed nap, Elizabeth was dressing for dinner as well as having a crisis of conscience.

She didn't know what she was doing here. Kristian didn't need a nurse, and he certainly didn't need the round-the-clock supervision her agency and staff had been providing.

How could she stay here? How could she take Cosima's money? It was not as if Kristian was even letting her do anything. He wanted to be in control—which was fine with her if he could truly motivate himself. He really would be better off with a sports trainer and an occupational therapist to help him adapt to his loss of sight rather than someone trained to deal with concussions, wounds, injuries and infections.

And, to compound her worry, she didn't have the foggiest idea how to dress for dinner.

She, who'd grown up in five-star hotels all over the world, was suffering a mild panic attack because she couldn't figure out what to wear for a late evening meal, at an old monastery, in the middle of the Taygetos.

One by one Elizabeth pulled out things from her wardrobe and discarded them. A swingy pleated navy skirt. Too school-girl. A straight brown gabardine skirt that nearly reached her ankles. She'd once thought it smart, but now she found it boring. A gray plaid skirt with a narrow velvet trim. She sighed, thinking they were all so serious and practical.

But wasn't that what she was supposed to be? Serious? Practical?

This isn't a holiday, she reminded herself sternly, retrieving the gray plaid skirt and pairing it with a pewter silk blouse. Dressing, she wrinkled her nose at her reflection. Ugh. So *not* pretty.

But why did she even care what she was wearing?

And that was when she felt a little wobble in her middle—butterflies, worry, guilt.

She was acting as if she was dressing for a dinner date instead of dinner with a patient. And that was wrong. Her being here, feeling this way, was wrong.

She was here for business. Medicine.

And yet as she remembered Kristian's smile by the pool, and his cool, mocking, "I thought we had a deal," she felt the wobble inside her again. And this time the wobble was followed by an expectant shiver.

She was nervous.

And excited.

And both emotions were equally inappropriate. Kristian was in her care. She'd been hired by his girlfriend to get him back on his feet. It would be professionally, never mind morally, wrong to think of him in any light other than as her patient.

A patient, she reminded herself.

Yet the butterflies in her stomach didn't go away.

With a quick, impatient flick of her wrist she dragged her brush through her hair. Kristian couldn't be an option even if he *was* single, and *not* her patient. It was ridiculous to romanticize or idealize him. She'd been married to a Greek and it had been a disaster from the start. Their marriage had lasted two years but scarred her for nearly seven.

The memory swept her more than ten years back, to when, as a twenty-year-old New York socialite, she had been toasted as the next great American beauty.

She'd been so young and inexperienced then, just a debutante entering the social scene, and she'd foolishly believed everything people told her. It would be three years before she fully understood that she was adored for her name and fortune, not for herself.

"No more Greek tycoons," she whispered to herself. "No more men who want you for the wrong reasons." Besides, marriage to a Greek had taught her that Mediterranean men preferred beautiful women with breasts and hips and hourglass figures—attributes slender, slim-hipped Elizabeth would never have.

With her hair a smooth pale gold curtain, she headed toward the library, since she didn't know where they were to eat tonight as the dining room had been converted into a fitness room.

Be kind, cordial, supportive, educational and useful, she told herself. But that is as far as your involvement goes.

Kristian entered the library shortly after she did. He was wearing dark slacks and a loose white linen shirt, and with his black hair combed back from his face his blue eyes seemed even more startling.

He wasn't happy, though, she thought, watching him push into the room, his wheelchair tires humming on the floor.

"Is something wrong?" she asked, still standing just inside the door, since she hadn't known where to go and didn't feel comfortable just sitting down. This was Kristian's refuge, after all, the place he spent the majority of his time.

He grimaced. "Now that I want to walk, I don't want to use the wheelchair."

"But you can't give up the chair yet. Though I bet you tried," she guessed, her tone sympathetic.

"I suppose I thought that, having stood, I could also probably walk."

"And you will. It'll take some time, but, considering your determination, it won't be as long as you think."

Pano appeared in the doorway to invite them to dinner. They followed him a short distance down the hall to a spacious room with a soaring ceiling hand-painted with scenes from the New Testament, in bold reds, blues, gray-greens and golds, although in places the paint was chipped and faded, revealing dark beams beneath.

A striking red wool carpet covered the floor, and in the middle of the carpet was a table set with two place-settings and two wood chairs. Fat round white candles glowed on the table and in sconces on the wall, and the dishes on the table were a glazed cobalt blue.

"It looks wonderful in here," she said, suddenly feeling foolish in her gray plaid skirt with its velvet trim. She should be wearing something loose and exotic—a flowing peasant skirt, a long jeweled top, even casual linen trousers came to mind. "The colors and artwork are stunning. This is the original ceiling, isn't it?"

"I had it saved."

"Is the building very old?"

"The tower dates to the 1700s while this part, the main monastery building, was put into service in 1802." Kristian drew a breath, held it, and just listened. After a moment he added more quietly. "Even though I can't see what's around me—the old stone walls, the beamed and arched ceilings. I feel it."

"That's good," she answered, feeling a tug on her heart. She could see why he loved the renovated monastery. It was atmospheric here, but it was so remote that she worried that Kristian wasn't getting enough contact with the outside world. He needed stimulation, interaction. He needed…a life.

But he's still healing, she reminded herself as they sat

down at the table, her place directly across from Kristian's. Just over a year ago he'd lost his brother, his cousin and numerous friends in the avalanche. He'd been almost fatally injured when his helicopter had crashed trying to look for survivors. Kristian had been badly hurt, and in the blunt trauma to his head he'd detached both retinas.

Sometimes, when she thought about it, it took her breath away just how much he'd lost in one day.

The housekeeper served the meal, and Pano appeared at Kristian's elbow, ready to assist him. Kristian sent him away. "We can manage," he said, reaching for the wine.

Kristian held the bottle toward Elizabeth, tilting it so she could read the label. "Will a glass hurt, Nurse Hatchet?"

His tone was teasing, but it was his expression which made her pulse quicken. He looked so boyish it disarmed her.

"A glass," she agreed cautiously.

He laughed and carefully reached out, found her glass, maneuvering the bottle so it was just over the rim. He poured slowly and listened carefully as he poured. "How is that?" he asked, indicating the glass. "Too much? Too little?"

"Just right."

He poured a glass for himself, before finding an empty spot on the table for the bottle.

The next course was almost immediately served, and he was attentive during the meal, asking her questions about work, her travels, her knowledge of Greek. "At one point I spent a lot of time in Greece," she answered, sidestepping any mention of her marriage.

"The university student on holiday?" Kristian guessed.

She made a face. "Everyone loves Greece."

"What do you like most about it?" he persisted.

A half-dozen different thoughts came to mind. The water.

The people. The climate. The food. The beaches. The warmth. But Greece had also created pain. So many people here had turned on her during her divorce. Friends—close friends—had dropped her overnight.

A lump filled her throat and she blinked to keep tears from forming. It was long ago, she told herself. Seven years. She couldn't let the divorce sour her on an entire country. Maybe her immediate social circle hadn't been kind when she and Nico separated, but not everyone was so judgmental or shallow.

"You've no answer?" he said.

"It's just that I like it all," she said, smiling to chase away any lingering sadness. "And you? What do you like best about your country?"

He thought about it for a moment, before lifting his wine glass. "The people. And their zest for life."

She clinked her glass against his, took another sip, and let the wine sit on her tongue a moment before swallowing. It was a red wine, and surprisingly good. She knew from the label it was Greek, but she wasn't as familiar with Greece's red wines as she was the white, as Nico preferred white. "Do you know anything about this wine?"

"I do. It's from one of my favorite wineries, a local winery, and the grape is *ayroyitiko,* which is indigenous to the Peloponnese."

"I didn't realize there were vineyards here."

"There are vineyards all over Greece—although the most famous Greek wines come from Samos and Crete."

"That's where you get the white wines, right?"

"Samian wine is, yes, and the most popular grape there is the *moshato.* Lots of wine snobs love Samian wine."

It was all she could do not to giggle. Nico, her former husband, was the ultimate wine snob. He'd go to a restaurant, order an outrageously priced bottle, and if he didn't think it up to snuff imperiously send it away. There had been times when Elizabeth had suspected there was absolutely nothing wrong with the wine. It was just Nico wanting to appear powerful.

"You're a white wine drinker?" Kristian asked.

"No, not really. I just had…friends…who preferred white Greek wine to red, so I'm rather ignorant when it comes to the different red grape varieties."

Kristian rested his forearms on the table. The corner of his mouth tugged. "A friend?" His expression shifted, suddenly perceptive. "A *male* friend?"

"He was male," she agreed carefully.

"And Greek?"

"And Greek."

He laughed softly, and yet there was tension in the sound, a hint that not all was well. "Greek men are sexual as well as possessive. I imagine your Greek friend wanted more from you than just friendship?"

Elizabeth blushed hotly. "It was a long time ago."

"It ended badly?"

Her head dipped. Her face burned. "I don't know." She swallowed, wondered why she was protecting Nico. "Yes," she corrected. "It did."

"Did this prejudice you against Greek men?"

"No." But she sounded uncertain.

"Against me?"

She blushed, and then laughed. "Maybe."

"So that is why I got the fleet of battleaxe nurses."

She laughed again. He amused her. And intrigued her. And if he wasn't her patient she'd even admit she found him very, very attractive. "Are you telling me you didn't deserve the battleaxe nurses?"

"I'm telling you I'm not like other Greek men."

Her breath suddenly caught in her throat, and her eyes grew wide. Somehow, with those words, he'd changed everything—the mood, the night, the meal itself. He'd charged the room with an almost unbearable electricity, a hot tension that made her fiercely aware of him. And herself. And the fact that they were alone together.

"You can't judge all wine based on one vintner or one bottle. And you can't judge Greek men based on one unhappy memory."

She felt as though she could barely breathe, and she struggled to find safer topics, ones that would allow her more personal distance. "What kind of wine do *you* like?"

"It's all about personal preference." He paused, letting his words sink in. "I like many wines. I have bottles in my cellar that are under ten euros which I think are infinitely more drinkable than some eighty-euro bottles."

"So it's not about the money?"

"Too many people get hung up on labels and names, and hope to impress each other with their spending power or their knowledge."

"We are talking about wine?" she murmured.

"Do you doubt it?" he asked, his head lifting as though to see her, study her, drink her in.

She bit into her lower lip, her cheeks so warm she felt desperate for a frozen drink or a sweet icy treat. Something to cool her off. Something to take her mind off Kristian's formidable physical appeal.

And, sitting there, she could see how someone like Calista, someone young and impressionable, might be attracted to Kristian. But to threaten him? Attempt to blackmail him? Impossible. Even blinded, with shattered bones and scarred features, he was too strong, too overpowering. Calista was a fool.

And, thinking of the girl's foolishness, Elizabeth began to giggle, and then her giggle turned into full blown laughter. "What was Calista thinking?" she wheezed, touching her hand to her mouth to try and stifle the sound, "How could someone like Calista think she could get away with blackmailing *you*?"

Kristian sat across the table from Elizabeth and listened to her laugh. It had been so long since he'd heard a laugh like that, so open and warm and real. Elizabeth in one day had made him realize how much he'd been missing in life. He hadn't even known he'd become so angry and shut down until she'd arrived and begun insisting on immediate changes.

He'd at first resented her bossy manner, but it had worked. He'd realized he didn't want or need someone else giving him orders, or attempting to dictate to him. There was absolutely no reason he couldn't motivate himself.

Although he was still incredibly suspicious of Cosima, and mistrusted her desire to have him walking and returning to Athens, he was also grateful for her interference. Cosima had brought Elizabeth here, and, as it turned out, Elizabeth was the right person at the right time.

He needed someone like her.

Maybe he even needed *her*.

Sitting across the table from her, he focused on where he pictured her to be sitting. He hoped she knew that even if he couldn't see, he was listening. Paying attention.

He'd never been known for his sensitivity. But it wasn't that he didn't have feelings. He just wasn't very good at expressing them.

He liked this room, and he was enjoying the meal. Even if he couldn't see, he appreciated the small touches made by

Pano and Atta, his housekeeper—like the low warm heat from the candles, which smelled faintly of vanilla.

He knew they were eating off his favorite plates. He could tell by the size and shape that they were the glazed ceramic dinnerware he'd bought several years ago at a shop on Santorini.

The weave and weight of the table linens made him suspect they were also artisan handicrafts—purchased impulsively on one of his trips somewhere.

Despite his tremendous wealth, Kristian preferred simplicity, and appreciated the talent of local artists, supporting them whenever he could.

"Now you've grown quiet," Elizabeth said, as Atta began clearing their dishes.

"I'm just relaxed," he said, and he was. It had been so long since he'd felt this way. Months and months since he'd experienced anything so peaceful or calm. He'd forgotten what it was like to share a meal with someone, had forgotten how food always tasted better with good conversation, good wine and some laughter.

"I'm glad."

The warm sincerity in her voice went all the way through him. He'd liked her voice even in the beginning, when she had insisted on calling him Mr. Koumantaros every other time she opened her mouth.

He also liked the scent she wore. He still didn't know what it was, although he could name all the other battleaxes' favorite fragrances: chlorine, antiseptic, spearmint, tobacco and, what was probably the worst of all, an annoyingly cloying rose-scented hand lotion.

Elizabeth also walked differently than the battleaxes. Her step was firm, precise, confident. He could almost imagine her sallying forth through a crowded store, decisive and determined as she marched through Fortnum and Mason's aisles.

He smiled a little, amused by this idea of her in London. That was where she lived. His smile faded as the silence stretched. He wished he could see her. He suddenly wondered if she was bored. Perhaps she wanted to escape, return to her room. She had passed on coffee.

As the seconds ticked by, Kristian's tension grew.

He heard Elizabeth's chair scrape back, heard her linen napkin being returned to the table. She was leaving.

Grinding his teeth, Kristian struggled to get to his feet. It was the second time in one day, and required a considerable effort, but Elizabeth was about to go and he wanted to say something—to ask her to stay and join him in the library. It was very possible she was tired, but for him the nights were long, sometimes endless. There was no difference between night and day anymore.

He was on his feet, gripping the table's edge with his fingers. "Are you tired?" he said, his voice suddenly too loud and hard. He hadn't meant to sound so brusque. It was uncertainty and the inability to read her mood that was making him harsh.

"A little," she confessed.

He inclined his head. "Goodnight, then."

She hesitated, and he wondered what she was thinking, wished he could see her face to know if there was pity or resentment or something else in her eyes. That was the thing about not being able to see. He couldn't read people the way he'd used to, and that had been his gift. He wasn't verbally expressive, but he'd always been intuitive. He didn't trust his intuition anymore, nor his instinct. He didn't know how to rely on either without his eyes.

"Goodnight," she said softly.

He dug his fingers into the linen-covered table. Nodded. Prayed she couldn't see his disappointment.

After another moment's hesitation he heard her footsteps go.

Slowly he sat back down in his wheelchair, and as he sat down something cracked in him. A second later he felt a lance of unbelievable pain.

How had he become so alone?

Gritting his teeth, he tried to bite back the loss and loneliness, but they played in his mind.

He missed Andreas. Andreas had been his brother, the last of his family. Their parents had died a number of years earlier—unrelated deaths, but they had come close together—and their deaths had brought he and Andreas, already close, even closer.

He should have saved Andreas first. He should have gone to his brother's aid first.

If only he could go back. If only he could undo that one decision.

In life there were so many decisions one took for granted—so many decisions one made under pressure—and nearly all were good decisions, nearly all were soon forgotten. It was the one bad decision that couldn't be erased. The one bad decision that stayed with you night and day.

Slowly he pushed away from the table, and even more slowly he rolled down the hall toward the library—the room he spent nearly all his waking hours in.

Maybe Pano could find something on the radio for him? Or perhaps there was an audio book he could listen to. Kristian just wanted something to occupy his mind.

But once in the library he stopped pushing and just sat near his table, with his papers and books. He didn't want the radio, and he didn't want to listen to a book on tape. He just wanted to be himself again. He missed who he was. He hated who he'd become.

"Kristian?" Elizabeth said timidly.

He straightened, sat taller. "Yes?"

"You're in here, then?"

"Yes. I'm right here."

"Oh." There was the faintest hitch in her voice. "It's dark. Do you mind if I turn the lights on?"

"No. Please. I'm sorry. I don't know—"

"Of course you don't know."

He heard her footsteps cross to the wall, heard her flip the switch and then approach. "I'm not really that sleepy, and I wondered if maybe you have something I could read to you. The newspaper, or mail? Maybe you even have a favorite book?"

Kristian felt some of the tension and darkness recede. "Yes," he said, exhaling gratefully. "I'm sure there is."

CHAPTER SEVEN

THAT night began a pattern they'd follow for the next two weeks. During the day Kristian would follow a prescribed workout regimen, and then in the evening he and Elizabeth would have a leisurely dinner, followed by an hour or two in the library, where she'd read to him from a book, newspaper or business periodical of his choice.

Kristian's progress astounded her. If she hadn't been there to witness the transformation, she wouldn't have believed it possible. But being here, observing the day-to-day change in Kristian, had proved once and for all that attitude was everything.

Every day, twice a day, for the past two weeks, Kristian had headed to the spacious dining room which had been converted into a rehabilitation room. Months ago the dining room's luxurious carpets had been rolled back, the furniture cleared out, and serious equipment had been hauled up the mountain face to dominate the space.

Bright blue mats covered the floor, and support bars had been built in a far corner to aid Kristian as he practiced walking. The nine windows overlooking the garden and valley below were always open, and Kristian spent hours at a time in that room.

The sports trainer Kristian had hired arrived two days after

Elizabeth did. Kristian had found Pirro in Sparta, and he had agreed to come and work with Kristian for the next four weeks, as long as he could return to Sparta on the weekends to be with his wife and children.

During the week, when Pirro was in residence, Kristian drove himself relentlessly. A trainer for the last Greek Olympic team, Pirro had helped rehabilitate and train some of the world's most elite athletes, and he treated Kristian as if he were the same.

The first few days Kristian did lots of stretching and developing core strength, with rubber balls and colored bands. By end of the first week he was increasing his distance in the pool and adding free weights to his routine. At the end of the second week Kristian was on cardio machines, alternating walking with short runs.

From the very beginning Elizabeth had known Kristian would get on his feet again. She hadn't expected it would only take him fifteen days.

Elizabeth stopped by the training room on Friday, early in the afternoon, to see if Pirro had any instructions for her for the two days while he returned to Sparta for the weekend.

She was shocked to see Kristian running slowly on a steep incline on the treadmill.

Pirro saw her enter and stepped over to speak with her. *"Ti Kanis?"* he asked. "How are you?"

"Kalo." Good. She smiled briefly before pointing to Kristian on the treadmill. "Isn't that a bit extreme?" she asked worriedly. "He could hardly stand two weeks ago. Won't the running injure him?"

"He's barely running," Pirro answered, glancing over his shoulder to watch Kristian's progress. "Notice the extreme incline? This is really a cross training exercise. Yes, we're working on increasing his cardio, but it's really to strengthen and develop the leg muscles."

Elizabeth couldn't help but notice the incline. Nor Kristian's intense concentration. He was running slowly, but without support, with his shoulders squared, his head lifted, his gaze fixed straight ahead. And even though sweat poured off him, and his cheeks glowed ruddy red, she didn't think he'd ever looked better—or stronger. Yes, he was breathing hard, but it was deep, regular, steady.

She walked closer to the machine, glanced at the screen monitoring his heart-rate. His heart-rate was low. She returned to Pirro's side. "So it's really not too much?" she persisted, torn between pride and anxiety. She wanted him better, but couldn't help fearing he'd burn out before he got to where he wanted to be.

"Too much?" Pirro grinned. "You don't know Kirie Kristian, do you? He's not a man. He's a monster."

Monster.

Pirro's word lingered in her mind as she turned to leave Kristian to finish his training. It was the same word Kristian had used when she'd first met him—the day he'd torn the bandages from his head to expose his face. Monster. Frankenstein.

Yet in the past two weeks he'd demonstrated that he was so far from either…

And so much more heroic than he even knew.

Soon he'd be returning to Athens. To the woman and the life that waited for him there. He'd eventually marry Cosima—apparently his family had known her forever—and with luck he'd have many children and a long, happy life.

But thinking of him returning to Athens put a heaviness in her heart. Thinking of him marrying Cosima made the heaviness even worse.

But that was why she was here, she reminded herself, swallowing hard around the painful lump in her throat, that lump that never went away. She'd come to prepare Kristian for the life he'd left behind.

And he was ready to go back. She could see it even if he couldn't.

The lump grew, thickening, almost drawing tears to her eyes.

Kristian, the Greek tycoon, had done this to her, too. She hadn't expected to feel this way about him, but he'd amazed her, impressed her, touched her heart with his courage, his sensitivity, as well as those rare glimpses of uncertainty. He made her feel so many emotions. But most of all he made her feel tender, good, hopeful, new. *New.*

"Shall I give him a message for you?" Pirro asked, his attention returning to Kristian.

And Elizabeth looked over at Kristian, this giant of a man who had surprised her at every level, her heart doing another one of those stunning free falls. He was so handsome it always touched a nerve, and that violent scar of his just made him more real, more beautiful. "No," she murmured. "There's no message. I'll just see him at dinner."

But as Elizabeth turned away, heading outside to take a walk through the gardens, she wondered when she'd find the courage to leave.

She had to leave. She'd already become too attached on him.

Putting a hand to her chest, she tried to stop the surge of pain that came with thinking of leaving.

Don't think of yourself, she reminded herself. Think of him. Think of his needs and how remarkable it is that he can do so much again. Think about his drive, his assertiveness, his ability to someday soon live independently.

And, thinking this way, she felt some of her own sadness

lifted. He and his confidence were truly amazing. You wouldn't know he couldn't see from the way he entered a room, or the way he handled himself. In the past couple of weeks he'd become more relaxed and comfortable in his own skin, and the more comfortable he felt, the more powerful his physical presence became.

She'd always known he was tall—easily over six feet two—but she'd never felt the impact of his height until he'd begun walking with a cane. Instead of stumbling, or hesitating, he walked with the assurance of a man who knew his world and fully intended to dominate that world once more.

Her lips curved in a rueful smile as she walked through the garden, with its low, fragrant hedges and rows of magnificent trees. No wonder a monastery had been built here hundreds of years ago. The setting was so green, the views breathtaking, the air pure and clean.

Pausing at one of the stone walls that overlooked the valley below, Elizabeth breathed in the scent of pine and lemon blossoms and gazed off into the distance, where the Messcnian plain stretched.

Kristian had told her that the Messenian plain was extraordinarily fertile and produced nearly every crop imaginable, including the delicious Kalamata olive. Beyond the agricultural plain was the sea, with what had to be more beautiful beaches and picturesque bays. Although Elizabeth had never planned on returning to Greece, now that she was here she was anxious to spend a day at the water. There was nothing like a day spent enjoying the beautiful Greek sun and sea.

"Elizabeth?"

Hearing her name called, she turned to discover Kristian heading toward her, walking through the gardens with his long narrow cane. He hadn't liked the cane initially, had said it emphasized his blindness, but once he'd realized the cane gave freedom as he learned to walk again, he had adapted to it with remarkable speed.

His pace was clipped, almost aggressive, bringing to mind a conversation she'd had with him a few days ago. She'd told him she was amazed by his progress and his confident stride. He'd shrugged the comment off, answering, "Greeks like to do things well or not at all."

She couldn't help smiling as she remembered his careless confidence, bordering on Greek arrogance. But it had been a truthful answer that suited him, especially now, as she watched him walk through the garden.

"Kristian, over here," she called to him, "I'm at the wall overlooking the valley."

It didn't take him long to reach her. He was still wearing the white short-sleeve T-shirt and gray baggy sweat pants he'd worked out in. His dark hair fell forward on his brow and his skin looked burnished with a healthy glow. Her gaze searched his face, looking for signs of exhaustion or strain. There were none. He just looked fit, relaxed, even happy.

"You had a grueling workout," she said.

"It was hard, but it felt good."

"Pirro can be brutal."

Kristian shrugged. "He knows I like to be challenged."

"But you feel okay?"

White teeth flashed and creases fanned from his eyes. "I feel great."

And there went her heart again, with that painful little flutter of attraction, admiration and sorrow. He wasn't hers. He'd never be hers. All she had to do was watch one of his exhausting physical therapy sessions to see that his desire to heal was for his Cosima. And although that knowledge stung, she knew before long she'd be back in her office and immersed in her administrative duties there.

The desk would be a good place for her. At her desk she'd be busy with the phone and computer and email. She wouldn't feel these disturbing emotions there.

"You were in the training room earlier," he said. "Everything all right?"

The soft breeze was sending tendrils of hair flying around her face, and she caught one and held it back by her ear. "I just wanted to check with Pirro—see if he had any instructions for me over the weekend."

"Did he?"

"No."

"I guess that means we've the weekend free."

"Are you making big plans, then?" she asked, teasing him, knowing perfectly well his routine didn't vary much. He was most confident doing things he knew, walking paths he'd become familiar with.

"I'm looking forward to dinner," he admitted.

"Wow. Sounds exciting."

The corner of his mouth lifted, his hard features softening at her gentle mockery. "Are you making fun of me?"

"Me? No. Never. You're Mr. Kristian Koumantaros—one of Greece's most powerful men—how could I even consider poking fun at you?"

"You would," he said, grooves paralleling his mouth. "You do."

"Mr. Koumantaros, you must be thinking of someone else."

"Mmm-hmm."

"I'm just a simple nurse, completely devoted to your wellbeing."

"Are you?"

"Of course. Have I not convinced you of that yet?" She'd meant to continue in her playful vein, but this time the words came out differently, her voice betraying her by dropping, cracking, revealing a tremor of raw emotion she didn't ever want him to hear.

Instead of answering, he reached out and touched her face. The unexpected touch shocked her, and she reared back, but his fingers followed, and slowly he slid his palm across her cheek.

The warmth in his hand made her face burn. She shivered at the explosion of heat within her even as her skin felt alive with bites of fire and ice.

"Kristian," she protested huskily, more heat washing through her—heat and need and something else. Something dangerously like desire.

She'd tried so hard to suppress these feelings, knowing if she acknowledged the tremendous attraction her control would shatter.

Her control *couldn't* shatter.

"No," she whispered, trying to turn her cheek away even as she longed to press her face to his hand, to feel more of the comfort and bittersweet pleasure.

She liked him.

She liked him very much. Too much. And, staring up into his face, she felt her fingers curl into her palm, fighting the urge to reach up and touch that beautiful scarred face of his.

Kristian, with his black hair and noble but scarred face, and his eyes that didn't see.

She began talking, to try to cover the sudden awkwardness between them. "These past two weeks you've made such great strides—literally, figuratively. You've no idea how proud I am of you, how much I admire you."

"That sounds suspiciously like a goodbye speech."

"It's not, but I *will* have to be leaving soon. You're virtually independent, and you'll soon be ready to return to your life in Athens."

"I don't like Athens."

"But your work—"

"I can do it here."

"But your family—"

"Gone."

She felt the tension between them grow. "Your friends," she said quietly, firmly. "And you do have those, Kristian. You have many people who miss you and want you back where you belong." Chief among them Cosima.

Averting his head, he stood tall and silent. His brows tugged and his jaw firmed, and slowly he turned his face toward her again. "When?"

"When what?"

"When do you intend to leave?"

She shrugged uncomfortably. "Soon." She took a quick breath. "Sooner than I expected."

"And when is that? Next week? The week after that?"

She twisted her fingers together. "Let's talk about this later."

"It's that soon?"

She nodded.

"Why?" he asked.

"It's work. I've a problem in Paris, and my case manager is fed up, threatening to walk off the job. I can't afford to lose her. I need to go and try to sort things out."

"So when is this? When do you plan to go?"

Elizabeth hesitated. "I was thinking about Monday." The lump was back in her throat, making it almost impossible to breathe. "After Pirro returns."

Kristian just stood there—big, imposing, and strangely silent.

"I've already contacted Cosima," she continued. "I told her that I've done all I can do and that it'd be wrong to continue to take her money." Elizabeth didn't add that she'd actually authorized her London office to refund Cosima's money, because it was Kristian who'd done the work, not she. It was Kristian's own miracle.

"Monday is just days away," Kristian said, his voice hard, increasingly distant.

"I know. It is sudden." She took a quick breath, feeling a stab of intense regret. She wished she could reach out and touch him, reassure him, but it wasn't her place. There were lines that couldn't be crossed, professional boundaries that she had to respect, despite her growing feelings for him. "You know you don't need me, Kristian. I'm just in your way—"

"No."

"Yes. But you must know I'm in awe of you. You said you'd walk in two weeks, and I said you couldn't. I said you'd need a walker, and you said you wouldn't." She laughed, thinking back to those first two intense and overwhelming days. "You've made a believer out of me."

He said nothing for a long moment, and then shook his head. "I wish I *could* make a believer out of you," he said, speaking so quietly the words were nearly inaudible.

"Monday is still three days from now," she said, injecting a note of false cheer. "Do we have to think about Monday today? Can't we think of something else? A game of blindman's bluff?"

Kristian's jaw drew tight, and then eased. He laughed most reluctantly. "You're a horrible woman."

"Yes, I know," she answered, grateful for humor.

"Most challenging, Cratchett."

"I'll take that as a compliment."

"Then you take it wrong."

Elizabeth smiled. When he teased her, when he played her game with her, it amused her to no end. Moments ago she'd felt so low, and yet she was comforted and encouraged now.

She loved his company. It was as simple as that. He was clever and sophisticated, handsome and entertaining. And once he'd determined to return to the land of the living, he had done so with a vengeance.

For the past week she'd tried to temper her happiness with reminders that soon he'd be returning to Athens, and marriage to Cosima, but it hadn't stopped her heart from doing a quick double-beat every time she heard his voice or saw him enter a room.

"I'm not sure of the exact time," Kristian said, "but I imagine it's probably close to five."

Elizabeth glanced at her silver watch. "It's ten past five now."

"I've made plans for dinner. It will mean dressing now. Can you be ready by six?"

"Is this for dinner here?"

"No."

"We're going *out?*" She gazed incredulously at the valley far below and the steep descent down. Sure, Pirro traveled up and down once a week to work with Kristian. But she couldn't imagine Kristian bumping around on the back of a mule or in a donkey's cart.

His expression didn't change. "Is that a problem?"

"No." But it kind of *was* a problem, she thought, glancing at the dwindling light. Where would they possibly go to eat? It would take them hours to get down the mountain, and it would be dark soon. But maybe Kristian hadn't thought of that, as his world was always dark.

Kristian heard the hesitation in Elizabeth's voice and he

tensed, his posture going rigid. He resented not being able to see her, particularly at times like this. It hadn't been until he couldn't see that he'd learned how much he'd depended on his eyes, on visual cues, to make decisions.

Why was she less than enthusiastic about dinner?

Did she not want to go with him? Or was she upset about something?

If only he could see her face, read her expression, he'd know what her hesitation meant. But, as it was, he felt as though he were stumbling blindly about. His jaw hardened. He hated this feeling of confusion and helplessness. He wasn't a helpless person, but everything was so different now, so much harder than before.

Like sleep.

And the nightmares that woke him up endlessly. Or, worse, the nightmares he couldn't wake from—the dreams that haunted him for hours when, even when he told himself to wake, even when he said in the dream, *This is just a dream,* he couldn't let go, couldn't open his eyes and see. Day or night, it was all the same. Black. Endless pitch-black.

"If you'd rather not go…" he said, his voice growing cooler, more distant. He couldn't exactly blame her if she didn't want another evening alone with him. She might say he didn't look like Frankenstein, but the scar on his face felt thick, and it ran at an angle, as though his face had been pieced together, stitched with rough thread.

"No, Kristian. No, that's not it at all," she protested, her hand briefly touching his arm before just as swiftly pulling away. And yet that light, faint touch was enough. It warmed him. Connected him. Made him feel real. And, God knew, between the darkness and the nightmares and the grief of losing Andreas, he didn't feel real, or good, very often anymore.

"I'd like to go," she continued. "I want to go. I just wasn't sure what to wear. Is there a dress code? Casual or elegant? How are you going to dress?"

He pressed the tip of his cane into the ground, wanting to touch her instead, wanting to feel the softness of her cheek, the silky texture that made him think of crushed rose petals and velvet and the softest lace edged satin. His body ached, his chest grew tight, pinched around his heart.

"I won't be casual." His voice came out rough, almost raw, and he winced. He'd developed edges and shadows that threatened to consume him. "But you should dress so that you're comfortable. It could be a late night."

In her bedroom, Elizabeth practically spun in circles.

They were going out, and it could be a late night. So where were they going and exactly how late was late?

Her stomach flipped over, and she felt downright giddy as she bathed and toweled off. It was ridiculous, preposterous to feel this way—and yet she couldn't help the flurry of excitement. It had been a little over two weeks since she'd arrived, and she was looking forward to dinner out.

Knowing that Kristian wouldn't be dressed casually, she flipped through her clothes in the wardrobe until she decided she'd wear the only dress she'd brought—a black cocktail-length dress with a pale lace inset.

Standing before the mirror, she blew her wet hair dry and battled to keep her chaotic emotions in check.

You're just his nurse, she reminded herself. Nothing more than that. But her bright eyes in the mirror and the quick beat of her pulse belied that statement.

Her hair shimmered. Elizabeth was going to leave it down, but worried she wouldn't appear professional. At the last minute she plaited her hair into two slender braids, then twisted the braids into an elegant figure-eight at the back of her head, before pulling some blonde wisps from her crown so they fell softly around her face.

Gathering a light black silk shawl and her small handbag, she headed for the monastery's library. As she walked through the long arched hallways she heard a distant thumping sound, a dull roar that steadily grew louder, until the sound was directly above and vibrating through the entire estate. Then abruptly the thumping stopped and everything was quiet again.

Elizabeth discovered Kristian already in the library, waiting for her.

He'd also showered and changed, was dressed now in elegant black pants and a crisp white dress shirt, with a fine leather black belt and black leather shoes. With his dark hair combed and his face cleanshaven, Elizabeth didn't think she'd ever met a man so fit, strong, or so darkly handsome.

"Am I underdressed?" he asked, lifting his hands as if to ask for her approval.

"No." Her heart turned over. God, he was beautiful. Did he have any idea how stunning he really was?

Kristian moved toward her, his cane folded, tucked under his arm. He looked so confident, so very sure of himself. "What are you wearing…besides high heels?"

"You could tell by the way I walked?" she guessed.

"Mmmm. Very sexy."

Blushing, she looked up into his face, glad he couldn't see the way she looked at him. She loved looking at him, and she didn't even know what she loved most about his face. It was just the way it came together—that proud brow, the jet-black eyebrows, the strong cheekbones above firm, mobile lips.

"I'm wearing a dress," she said, feeling suddenly shy. She'd never been shy around men before—had never felt intimidated by any man, not even her Greek former husband. "It's black velvet with some lace at the bodice. Reminds me of the 1920s flapper-style dress."

"You must look incredible."

The compliment, as well as the deep sincerity in Kristian's voice, brought tears to her eyes.

Kristian was so much more than any man she'd ever met. It wasn't his wealth or sophistication that impressed her, either—although she did admit that he wore his clothes with ease and elegance, and she'd heard his brilliant trading and investments meant he'd tripled his family fortune—those weren't qualities she respected, much less admired.

She liked different things—simple things. Like the way his voice conveyed so much, and how closely he listened to her when she talked to him. His precise word choice indicated he paid attention to virtually everything.

"Not half as incredible as you do," she answered.

His mouth quirked. "Ready?"

"Yes."

He held out his arm and she took it. His body was so much bigger than hers, and warm, the muscles in his arm dense and hard. Together they headed through the hall to the front entrance, where Pano stood, ready to open the front door.

At the door Kristian paused briefly, head tipped as he gazed down at her. "Your chariot awaits," he said, and with another step they crossed the monastery's threshold and went outside—to a white and silver helicopter.

CHAPTER EIGHT

A HELICOPTER.

On the top of one of Taygetos's peaks.

She blinked, shook her head, and looked again, thinking that maybe she'd imagined it. But, no, the silver and white body glinted in the last rays of the setting sun.

"I wondered how you got up and down the mountain," she said. "You didn't seem the type to enjoy donkey rides."

Kristian's deep laugh hummed all the way through her. "I suppose I could have sent the helicopter for you."

"No, no. I would have hated to miss hours bumping and jolting around in a wood cart.

He laughed again, as though deeply amused. "Have you been in a helicopter before?"

"I have," she said. "Yes." Her parents had access to a helicopter in New York. But that was part of the affluent life she'd left behind. "It's been a while, though."

The pilot indicated they were safe to board, and Elizabeth walked Kristian to the door. Once on board, he easily found his seatbelt and fastened the clip. And it wasn't until they'd lifted off, heading straight up and then over, between the mountain peaks, that Elizabeth remembered that the worst of

Kristian's injuries had come from the helicopter crash instead of the actual avalanche.

Turning, she glanced into his face to see what he was feeling. He seemed perhaps a little paler than he had earlier, but other than that he gave no indication that anything was wrong.

"You were hurt in a helicopter accident," she said, wondering if he was really okay, or just putting up a brave front.

"I was."

She waited, wondering if he'd say more. He didn't, and she touched the tip of her tongue to her upper lip. "You're not worried about being in one now?"

His brows pulled. "No. I know Yanni the pilot well—very well—and, being a pilot myself…"

"You're a pilot?"

His dark head inclined and he said slowly, "I was flying at the time of the crash."

Ah. "And the others?" she whispered.

"They were all in different places and stages of recovery." His long black lashes lowered, hiding the brilliant blue of his eyes.

She waited, and eventually Kristian sighed, shifted, his broad shoulders squaring. "One had managed to ski down the mountain to a lower patrol. Cosima…" He paused, took a quick short breath. "Cosima and the guide had been rescued. Two were still buried in snow and the others…were located but already gone."

The details were still so vague, and his difficulty in re-counting the events so obvious that she couldn't ask anything else. But there were things she still wanted to know. Like, had he been going back for his brother when he crashed? And how had he managed to locate Cosima so quickly but not Andreas?

Thinking of the accident, she stole a swift side-glance in Kristian's direction. Yes, he was walking, and, yes, he was physically stronger. But what if he never saw again?

What if he didn't get the surgery—or, worse, did have it and the treatment didn't work? What if his vision could never be improved? What then?

She actually thought Kristian would cope—it wouldn't be easy, but he was tough, far tougher than he'd ever let on—but she wasn't so sure about Cosima, because Cosima desperately wanted Kristian to be "normal" again. And those were Cosima's words: "He must be normal, the way he was, or no one will ever respect him."

How would Cosima feel if Kristian never did get his sight back?

Would she still love him? Stay with him? Honor him?

Troubled, Elizabeth drew her shawl closer to her shoulders and gazed out the helicopter window as they flew high over the Peloponnese peninsula. It was a stunning journey at sunset, the fading sun painting the ground below in warm strokes of reddish-gold light.

In her two years of living in Greece she'd never visited the Peloponnese. Although the Peloponnese was a favorite with tourists, for its diverse landscape and numerous significant archeological sites, she only knew what Kristian had been telling her these past couple weeks. But, remembering his tales, she was riveted by three "fingers" of land projecting into the sea, the land green and fertile against the brilliant blue Mediterranean.

"We're almost there," Kristian suddenly said, his hand briefly touching her knee.

She felt her stomach flip and, breath catching, she glanced down at her knee, which still felt the heat of his fingers even though his hand was no longer there.

She wanted him to touch her again. She wanted to feel his hand slide inside her knee, wanted to feel the heat of his hand, his palm on her knee, and then feel his touch slide up the inside of her thigh. And maybe it couldn't happen, but it didn't make the desire any less real.

Skin against skin, she thought. Touch that was warm and concrete instead of all these silent thoughts and intense emotions. And they were getting harder to handle, because she couldn't acknowledge them, couldn't act on them, could do nothing but keep it in, hold it in, pretend she wasn't falling head over heels in love. Because she was.

And it was torture. Madness.

Her heart felt like it was tumbling inside her chest—a small shell caught in the ocean tide. She couldn't stop it, couldn't control it, could only feel it.

With an equally heart-plunging drop, the helicopter descended straight down.

As the pilot opened the door and assisted her and then Kristian out, she saw the headlights of a car in front of them. The driver of the car stepped out, and as he approached she realized it was Kristian's driver.

Whisked from helicopter to car, Elizabeth slid through the passenger door and onto the leather seat, pulse racing. Her pulse quickened yet again as Kristian climbed in and sat close beside her.

"Where are we?" she asked, feeling the press of Kristian's thigh against hers as the driver set off.

"Kithira."

His leg was much longer than hers, his knee extending past hers, the muscle hard against hers.

"It's an island at the foot of the Peloponnese," he added. "Years ago, before the Corinth Canal was built in the late nineteenth century, the island was prosperous due to all the ships stopping. But after the canal's construction the island's population, along with its fortune, dwindled."

As the car traveled on quiet roads, beneath the odd passing yellow light, shadows flickered in and through the windows. Elizabeth couldn't tear her gaze from the sight of his black trouser-covered leg against hers.

"It's nice to be going out," he said, as the car began to wind up a relatively steep hill. "I love living in the Taygetos, but every now and then I just want to go somewhere for dinner, enjoy a good meal and not feel so isolated."

She turned swiftly to look at him. There were no street-lights on the mountain road and she couldn't see his face well. "So you *do* feel isolated living so far from everyone?"

He shrugged. "I'm Greek."

Those two words revealed far more than he knew. Greeks treasured family, had strong ties to family, even the extended family, and every generation was respected for what it contributed. In Greece the elderly rarely lived alone, and money was never hoarded, but shared with each other. A father would never let his daughter marry without giving her a house, or land, or whatever he could, and a Greek son would always contribute to his parents' care. It wasn't just an issue of respect, but love.

"That's why Cosima wants you back in Athens," Elizabeth said gently. "There you have your *parea*—your group of friends." And, for Greeks, the circle of friends was nearly as important as family. A good *parea* was as necessary as food and water.

But Kristian didn't speak. Elizabeth, not about to be put off, lightly touched his sleeve. "Your friends miss you."

"My *parea* is gone."

"No—"

"Elizabeth." He stopped her. "They're gone. They died with my brother in France. All those that perished, suffocating in the snow, were my friends. But they weren't just friends. They were also colleagues."

Pained, she closed her eyes. Why, oh why did she push? Why, oh, why did she think she knew everything? How could she be so conceited as to think she could counsel him? "I'm sorry."

"You didn't know."

"But I thought… Cosima said…"

"Cosima?" Kristian repeated bitterly. "Soon you will learn you can't believe everything she says."

"Even though she means well."

Silence filled the car, and once again Elizabeth sensed that she'd said the wrong thing. She pressed her fists to her knees, increasingly uncomfortable.

"Perhaps I should tell you about dinner," Kristian said finally, his deep chest lifting as he squared his shoulders. "We're heading to a tiny village that will seem virtually untouched by tourism or time. Just outside this village is one of my favorite restaurants—a place designed by a Greek architect and his artist wife. The food is simple, but fresh, and the view is even better."

"You could go anywhere to eat, but you choose a rustic and remote restaurant?"

"I like quiet places. I'm not interested in fanfare or fuss."

"Have you always been this way, or…?"

"It's not the result of the accident, no. Andreas was the extrovert—he loved parties and the social scene."

"You didn't go with him?"

"Of course I went with him. He was my brother and my best friend. But I was content to let him take center stage, entertain everyone. It was more fun to sit back, watch."

As Kristian talked, the moon appeared from behind a cloud. Elizabeth could suddenly see Kristian's features, and that rugged profile of his, softened only by the hint of fullness at his lower lip.

He had such a great mouth, too. Just wide enough, with perfect lips.

To kiss those lips…

Knots tightened inside her belly, knots that had less to do with fear and more to do with desire. She felt so attracted to him it was hard to contain her feelings, to keep the need from showing.

What she needed to do was scoot over on the seat, put some distance between them—because with him sitting so close, with their thighs touching and every now and then their elbows brushing, she felt so wound up, so keenly aware of him.

She looked now at his hand, where it rested on his thigh, and she remembered how electric it had felt when his hand had brushed her knee, how she'd wanted his hand to slide beneath the hem of her dress and touch her, tease her, set her on fire…

That hand. His body. Her skin.

She swallowed hard, her heart beating at a frantic tempo, and, crossing her legs, she fought the dizzying zing of adrenaline. This was ridiculous, she told herself, shifting again, crossing her legs the other way. She had to settle down. Had to find some calm.

"You seem restless," Kristian said, head cocking, listening attentively.

She pressed her knees together. "I guess I am. I probably just need to stretch my legs. Must be the sitting."

"We're almost there."

"I'm not complaining."

"I didn't think you were."

She forced a small tight smile even as her mind kept spinning, her imagination working overtime. She was far too aware of Kristian next to her, far too aware of his warmth, the faint spice of his cologne or aftershave, the formidable size of him…even the steady way he was breathing.

"You're not too tired, are you?" he asked as the car headlights illuminated the road and what seemed to be a nearly barren slope before them.

"No," she said, as the car suddenly turned, swinging onto a narrow road.

"Hungry?"

She made a soft sound and anxiously smoothed the velvet hem of her dress over her knees. "No. *Yes*. Could be." She laughed, yet the sound was apprehensive. "I honestly don't know what's wrong with me."

He reached out, his hand finding hers in the dark with surprising ease. She thought for a moment he meant to hold her hand but instead he turned it over and put his fingers on the inside of her wrist, checking her pulse. Several seconds passed before his mouth quirked. "Your heart's racing."

"I know," she whispered, staring at her wrist in his hand as the lights of a parking lot and restaurant illuminated the car. His hand was twice the size of her own, and his skin, so darkly tanned, made hers look like cream.

"You're not scared of me?"

"No."

"But maybe you're afraid to be alone with me?"

Her heart drummed even harder, faster. "And why would that be?"

His thumb caressed her sensitive wrist for a moment before releasing her. "Because tonight you're not my nurse, and I'm not your patient. We're just two people having dinner together."

"Just friends," she said breathlessly, tugging her hand free, suddenly terrified of everything she didn't know and didn't understand.

"Can a man and a woman be just friends?"

Elizabeth's throat seized, closed.

The driver put the car into "park" and came around to open their door. Elizabeth nearly jumped from the car, anxious to regain control.

At the restaurant entrance they were greeted as though they were family, the restaurant owner clasping Kristian by the arms and kissing him on each cheek. "Kyrios Kristian," he said, emotion thickening his Greek. "*Kyrie*. It is good to see you."

Kristian returned the embrace with equal warmth. "It is good to be back."

"*Parakalo*—come." And the older man, his dark hair only peppered with gray, led them to a table in a quiet alcove with windows all around. "The best seats for you. Only the best for you, my son. Anything for you."

After the owner left, Elizabeth turned to Kristian. "He called you *son?*"

"The island's small. Everyone here is like family."

"So you know him well?"

"I used to spend a lot of time here."

She glanced out the window and the view was astonishing. They were high on a hill, perched above a small village below. And farther down from the village was the ocean.

The lights of the village twinkled and the moon reflected off the white foam of the sea, where the waves broke on the rocks and shore.

The restaurant owner returned, presenting them with a gift—a bottle of his favorite wine—pouring both glasses before leaving the bottle behind.

"*Yiassis*," she said, raising her glass and clinking it with his. *To your health.*

"*Yiassis*," he answered.

And then silence fell, and the stillness felt wrong. Something was wrong. She just knew it.

Kristian shifted, and a small muscle suddenly pulled in his cheek. Elizabeth watched him, feeling a rise in tension.

The mood at the table was suddenly different.

Kristian suddenly seemed so alone, so cut off in his world. "What's wrong?" she asked nervously, fearing that she'd said something, done something to upset him.

He shook his head.

"Did I do something?" she persisted.

"No."

"Kristian." Her tone was pleading. "Tell me."

His jaw worked, the hard line of his cheekbone growing even more prominent, and he laughed, the sound rough and raw. "I wish to God I could see you."

For a moment she didn't know what to say or do, as heat rushed through her. And then the heat receded, leaving her chilled. "Why?" she whispered.

"I just want to see you."

Her face grew hot all over again, and this time the warmth stayed, flooding her limbs, making her feel far too sensitive. "Why? I'm just another battleaxe."

"Ohi." No. "Hardly."

Her hand shook as she adjusted her silverware. "You don't know that—"

"I know how you sound, and smell. I know you barely reach my shoulder—even in heels—and I know how your skin feels—impossibly smooth, and soft, like the most delicate satin or flower."

"I think you've found your old pain meds."

His dark head tipped. His blue eyes fixed on her. "And I think you're afraid of being with me."

"You're wrong."

"Am I?"

"Yes." She reached for her water glass and took a quick sip of the bubbly mineral water, but drank so much that the bubbles ended up stinging her nose. "I'm not afraid," she said, returning the glass to a table covered in white crisp linen and flickering with soft ivory candlelight and shadows. "How could I be afraid of you?"

His lips barely curved. "I'm not nice, like other men."

Her heart nearly fell. She looked up at him from beneath her lashes. "I'm not going to even dignify that with a response."

"Why?"

"Because you're baiting me," she said.

He surprised her by laughing. "My clever girl."

Her heart jumped again, and an icy hot shiver raced through her. Liquid fire in her veins. *His clever girl.* He was torturing her now. Making her want to be more than she was, making her want to have more than she did. Not more things, but more love.

His love.

But he was promised, practically engaged. And she'd been through hell and back with one man who hadn't been able to keep his word, or honor his commitments. Including his marriage vows.

"Kristian, I can't do this." She would have gotten up and run if there had been anywhere to go. "I can't play these games with you."

His forehead furrowed, emphasizing the scar running down his cheek. "What games?"

"These…this…whatever you call this. Us." She shook her head, unable to get the words out. "I know what you said earlier, that tonight we're not patient and nurse, we're just a man and…woman. But that's not right. You're wrong. I *am* your nurse. That's all I am, all I can be."

He leaned back and rested one arm on the table, his hand relaxed. His expression turned speculative. "And will you still be my nurse when you return to London in two days?"

"Three days."

"Two days."

She held her breath, her fingers balling into fists and then slowly exhaled.

His mouth tugged and lines deepened near his lips, emphasizing the beautiful planes of his face. "Elizabeth, *latrea mou,* let us not play games, as you say. Why do you have to go back?"

"I have a business to run—and, Kristian, so do you. Your officers and board of directors are desperate for you to return to Athens and take leadership again."

"I can do it from Taygetos."

She shook her head, impatient. "No, you can't. Not properly. There are appointments, conferences, press meetings—"

"Others can do it," he said dismissively.

Staring at him, she felt her frustration grow. He'd never sounded so arrogant as he did now. "But *you* are Koumantaros. You are the one investors believe in and the one your business partners want to meet with. *You* are essential to Koumantaros Incorporated's success."

He nearly snapped his fingers, rejecting her arguments. "Did Cosima put you up to this?"

"No. Of course not. And that's not the issue here anyway. The issue is you resuming your responsibilities."

"Elizabeth, I still head the corporation."

"But absent leadership?" She made a soft scoffing sound. "It's not effective, and, frankly, it's not you."

"How can one little Englishwoman have so many opinions about things she knows so little about?"

Elizabeth's cheeks flamed. "I know you better than you think," she flashed.

"I'm referring to the corporate world—"

"I am a business owner."

It was his turn to scoff. "Which we've already established isn't well managed at all."

Hurt, she abruptly drew back and stared at him. "That was unkind. And unnecessary."

He shrugged off her rebuke. "But true. Your agency provided me with exceptionally poor care. Propositioned and then blackmailed by one nurse, and demeaned by the others."

She threw her napkin down and pushed her chair back. "Maybe you were an exceptionally poor patient."

"Is that possible?"

"Possible?" she repeated, her voice quavering with anger and indignation. "My God, you're even more conceited than I dreamed. *Possible?*" She drew a swift breath. "Do you want the truth? No more sugar-coated words?"

"Don't start mincing words now," he drawled, sounding as bored as he looked.

Her fingers flexed, and blood pumped through her veins. She wanted to smack him, she really did. "Truth, Kristian— *you* were impossible. You were the worst patient in the history of my agency, and we take care of hundreds of patients every year. I've had my business for years, and never encountered anyone as self-absorbed and manipulative as you."

She took another quick breath. "And another thing—do you think I *wanted* to leave my office, put aside my obligations, to rush to your side? Do you think this was a holiday for me to come to Greece? No. And no again. But I did it because no one else would, and you had a girlfriend desperate to see you whole and well."

Legs shaking, Elizabeth staggered to her feet. "Speaking of your girlfriend, it's time you gave her a call. I'm done here. It's Cosima's turn to be with you now!"

CHAPTER NINE

ELIZABETH rushed out of the restaurant, past the three other tables of patrons. But no sooner had she stepped outside into the decidedly cooler night air than she felt assailed by shame. She'd just walked out on Kristian Koumantaros, one of Greece's most powerful and beloved tycoons.

As gusts of wind whistled past the building, perched on the mountain edge, she hugged her arms close, chilled, overwhelmed. She'd left a man who couldn't see alone, to find his own way out. And worst of all, she thought, tugging windblown tendrils behind her ears, she'd left in the middle of the meal. Meals were almost as sacred as family in Greece.

She was falling apart, she thought, putting a hand to her thigh to keep her skirt from billowing out. Her feelings were so intense she was finding it difficult to be around Kristian. She was overly emotional and too sensitive. And this was why she had to leave—not because she couldn't still do good here, but because she wondered if she couldn't manage her own emotions, how could she possibly help him manage his?

In London things would be different.

In London she wouldn't see Kristian.

In London she'd be in control.

A bitter taste filled her mouth and she immediately shook

her head, unable to bear the thought that just days from now she'd be gone and he'd be out of her life.

How could she leave him?

And yet how could she remain?

In the meantime she was standing outside Kristian's favorite restaurant while he sat alone inside. God, what a mess.

She had to go back in there. Had to apologize. Try to make amends before the evening was completely destroyed.

With a deep breath, she turned and walked through the front door, out of the night which was rapidly growing stormy. Chilly. She rubbed at her arms and returned to their table, where Kristian waited.

He was sitting still, head averted, and yet from his profile she could see his pallor and the strain at his jaw and mouth.

He was as upset as she was.

Heart sinking, Elizabeth sat down. "I'm sorry," she whispered, fighting the salty sting of tears. "I'm sorry. I don't know what else to say."

"It's not your fault. Don't apologize."

"Everything just feels wrong—"

"It's not you. It's me." His dense black lashes dropped. He hesitated, as though trying to find the right words. "I knew you'd need to go back, but I didn't expect you'd say it was so soon—didn't expect the announcement today."

She searched his face. It was a face she loved. *Loved.* And while the word initially took her by surprise, she also recognized it was true. "Kristian, I'm not leaving *you.* I'm just returning to my office and the work that awaits me there."

He hesitated a long time before picking up his wine glass, but setting it back down without taking a drink. "You couldn't move your office here?"

"Temporarily?"

"Permanently."

She didn't understand. "I didn't make this miracle, Kristian. It was you. It was your focus, your drive, your hours of work—"

"But I didn't care about getting better, didn't care about much of anything, until *you* arrived. And now I do."

"That's because you're healing."

"So don't leave while I'm still healing. Don't go when everything finally feels good again."

She closed her eyes, hope and pain streaking through her like twin forks of lightning. "But if I move my office here, if I remain here to help you…"

"Yes?"

She shook her head. "What about me? What happens to me when you're healed? When you're well?" She was grateful he couldn't see the tears in her eyes, or how she was forced to madly dash them away before anyone at the restaurant could see. "Once you've gotten whatever you need from me, do I just pack my things and go back to London again?"

He said nothing, his expression hard, grim.

"Kristian, forgive me, but sometimes being here in Greece is torture." She knotted her hands in her lap, thinking that the words were coming out all wrong but he had to realize that, while she didn't want to hurt him, she also had to protect herself. She was too attached to him already. Leaving him, losing him, would hurt so much. But remaining to watch him reunite with another woman would break her heart. "I like you, Kristian," she whispered. "Really like you—"

"And I like you. Very much."

"It's not the same."

"I don't understand. I don't understand any of this. I only know what I think. And I believe you belong here. With me."

He was saying words she'd wanted to hear, but not in the context she needed them. He wanted her because she was convenient and helpful, supportive while still challenging. Yet the relationship he was describing wasn't one of love, but usefulness. He wanted her company because it would benefit him. But how would *she* benefit by staying?

"Elizabeth, *latrea mou,*" he added, voice deepening. "I need you."

Latrea mou. Darling. Devoted one.

His voice and words were buried inside her heart. Again tears filled her eyes, and again she was forced to brush them swiftly away. "No wonder you had mistresses on every continent," she said huskily. "You know exactly what women want to hear."

"You're changing the subject."

She wiped away another tear. "I'm making an observation."

"It's not accurate."

"Cosima said—"

"This isn't working, is it? Let's just go." Kristian abruptly rose, and even before he'd straightened the restaurant owner had rushed over. "I'm sorry," Kristian apologized stiffly, his expression shuttered. "We're going to be leaving."

"*Kyrie,* everything is ready. We're just about to carry out the plates," the owner said, clasping his hands together and looking from one to the other. "You are sure?"

Kristian didn't hesitate. "I am sure." He reached into his pocket, retrieved his wallet and cash. "Will you let my driver know?"

"Yes, Kyrie Kristian." The other man nodded. "At least let me have your meal packed to go. Maybe later you will be hungry and want a little plate of something, yes?"

"Thank you."

Five minutes later they were in the car, sitting at opposite ends of the passenger seat as the wind gusted and howled outside. Fat raindrops fell heavily against the windshield. Kristian stonily faced forward while Elizabeth, hands balled against her stomach, stared out the car window at the passing scenery, although most of it was too dark to see.

She didn't understand what had happened in the restaurant tonight. Everything had been going so well until they'd sat down, and then...

And then...what? Was it Cosima? Her departure? What?

As the car wound its way back down the mountain, she squeezed her knuckled fists, her insides a knot of regret and disappointment. The evening was a disaster, and she'd been so excited earlier, too.

"What happened?" she finally asked, breaking the miserably tense silence. "Everything seemed fine in the helicopter."

He didn't answer and, turning, she looked at him, stared at him pointedly, waiting for him to speak. He had to talk. He had to communicate.

But he wouldn't say a word. He sat there, tall, dark, impossibly remote, as though he lived in a different world.

"Kristian," she whispered. "You're being horrible. Don't do this. Don't be like this—"

His jaw hardened and his lashes flickered, but that was his only response, and she thought she could hate him in that moment—hate him not just now, but forever.

To be shut out, to be ignored. It was the worst punishment she could think of. So unbelievably hard to bear.

"The weather is going to be a problem," he said at last. "We won't be able to fly. Unfortunately we are unable to return to Taygetos tonight. We'll be staying in the capital city, Chora."

The driver had long ago merged with traffic, driving into

and through a harbor town. If this was the capital city it wasn't very big. They were now paralleling the coast, passing houses, churches and shops, nearly all already closed for the night. And far off in the distance a vast hulking fortress dwarfed the whitewashed town.

As the windshield wipers rhythmically swished, Elizabeth gazed out the passenger window, trying to get a better look at the fortress. It sat high above the city, on a rock of its own. In daylight the fortress would have an amazing view of the coast, but like the rest of Chora it was dark now, and even more atmospheric, with the rain slashing down.

"You've booked us into a hotel?" she asked, glimpsing a church steeple inside the miniature walled town.

"We won't be at a hotel. We'll be staying in a private home."

She glanced at him, her feelings still hurt. "Friends?"

"No. It's mine." He shifted wearily. "My home. One of my homes."

They were so close to the fortress she could see the distinct stones that shaped the mammoth walls. "Are we far from your home?"

"I don't think so, no. But I confess I'm not entirely sure where we are at the moment."

Of course—he couldn't see. And he wouldn't automatically know which direction they were going, or the current road they were traveling on. "We're heading toward a castle."

"Then we're almost there."

"We're staying near the castle?"

"We're staying *at* the castle."

"Your home is a castle?"

"It's one of my properties."

Her brows pulled. "How many properties do you have?"

"A few."

"Like this?"

"They're all a bit different. The monastery in Taygetos, the castle here, and other estates in other places."

"Are they all so…grand?"

"They're all historic. Some are in ruins when I purchase them; some are already in operation. But that's what I do. It's one of the companies in the Koumantaros portfolio. I buy historic properties and find different ways to make them profitable."

Elizabeth turned her attention back to the fortress, with its thick walls and towers and turrets looming before them. "And this is a real castle?"

"Venetian," he agreed. "Begun in the thirteenth century and finished in the fifteenth century."

"So what do you do with it?"

He made a soft, mocking sound. "My accountants would tell you I don't do enough, that it's an enormous drain on my resources, but after purchasing it three years ago I couldn't bear to turn it into a five-star luxury resort as planned."

"So you stay here?"

"I've reserved a wing for my private use, but I haven't visited since before the accident."

"So it essentially sits empty?"

The wind suddenly howled, and rain buffeted the car. Elizabeth didn't know if it was the weather or her question, but Kristian smiled faintly. "You're sounding like my accountants now. But, no, to answer your question. It's not empty. I've been working with an Italian architect and designer to slowly—carefully—turn wings and suites into upscale apartments. Two suites are leased now. By next year I hope to lease two or three more, and then that's it."

The car slowed and then stopped, and an iron gate

opened. The driver got out and came round to open their door. "We're here."

A half-dozen uniformed employees appeared from nowhere. Before Elizabeth quite understood what was happening, she was being whisked in one direction and Kristian in another.

Left alone in an exquisite suite of rooms, she felt a stab of confusion.

Where on earth was she now?

The feeling was strongly reminiscent of how she'd been as a child, the only daughter of Rupert Stile, the fourth richest man in America, as she and her parents had traveled from one sumptuous hotel to the next.

It wasn't that they hadn't had houses of their own—they'd had dozens—but her mother had loved accompanying her father on his trips, and so they had all traveled together, the young heiress and her nannies too.

Back then, though, she hadn't Elizabeth Hatchet but Grace Elizabeth Stiles, daughter of a billionaire a hundred times over. It had been a privileged childhood, made only more enviable when she had matured from pampered daughter status to being the next high-society beauty.

Comfortable in the spotlight, at ease with the media, she'd enjoyed her debutante year and the endless round of parties. Invitations had poured in from all over the world, as had exquisite designer clothes made for her specifically.

It had been so much power for a twenty-year-old. Too much. She'd had her own money, her own plane, and her own publicist. When men wined her and dined her—and they *had* wined and dined her—the dates had made tabloid news.

Enter handsome Greek tycoon Nico. Being young, she'd had no intention of settling down so soon, but he'd swept her off her feet. Dazzled her completely with attention, affection, tender gifts and more. Within six months they'd been engaged. At twenty-three she'd had the fairytale wedding of her dreams.

Seven and a half months after her wedding she had discovered him in bed with another woman.

She'd stayed with him because he'd begged for another chance, promised to get counseling, vowed he'd change. But by their first anniversary he'd cheated again. And again. And again.

The divorce had been excruciating. Nico had demanded half her wealth and launched a public campaign to vilify her. She was selfish, shallow, self-absorbed—a spoiled little rich girl intent on controlling him and embarrassing him. She'd emasculated him by trying to control the purse strings. She'd refused to have conjugal relations.

By the time the settlement had been reached, she hadn't been able to stand herself. She wasn't any of the things Nico said, and yet the public believed what they were told—or maybe she'd begun to believe the horribly negative press, too. Because by the end, Grace detested her name, her fortune, and the very public character assassination.

Moving to England, she'd changed her name, enrolled in nursing school and become someone else—someone stable and solid and practical.

But now that same someone was back in Greece, and the two lives felt very close to colliding.

She should have never returned to Greece—not even under the auspices of caring for a wounded tycoon. She definitely shouldn't have taken a helicopter ride to a small Greek island. And she definitely, *definitely* shouldn't have agreed to stay in a thirteenth-century castle in the middle of a thunderstorm.

Exhausted, Elizabeth pivoted slowly in her room like a

jewelry box ballerina. Where had Kristian gone? Would she see him again tonight? Or was she on her own until morning?

As if on cue, the bedroom lights flickered once, twice, and then went out completely, leaving her in darkness.

At first Elizabeth did nothing other than move toward the bed and sit there, certain at any moment the power would come back on or one of the castle staff would appear at her room, flashlight, lantern or candle in hand. Neither happened. No power and no light. Minutes dragged by. Minutes that became longer.

Unable even to read her own watch, Elizabeth didn't know how much time had gone by, but she thought it had to have been nearly an hour. She was beyond bored, too. She was hungry, and if no one was coming to her assistance, then she would go to them.

Stumbling her way toward the door, she bumped into a trunk at the foot of the bed, a chair, a table—ouch—the wall, tapestry on the wall, and finally a door.

The hall was even darker than her room. Not a flicker of light anywhere, nor a sound.

A rational woman would return to her room and call it a night, but Elizabeth was too hungry—and a little too panicked—to be rational, and, taking a left from her room, began a slow, fearful walk down the hall, knowing there were stairs somewhere up ahead but not certain how far away, nor how steep the staircase. She couldn't even remember if there was one landing or two.

Just when she thought she'd found the stairs she heard a noise. And it wasn't the creak of stairs or a door opening, but something live, something breathing. Whimpering.

She stopped dead in her tracks. Her heart raced and, reaching for the wall, her hand shook, her skin icy and clammy.

There was something—someone—in the stairwell, something—someone—waiting.

She heard a heavy thump, and then silence. Ears, senses straining, she listened. It was breathing harder, heavier, and there was another thump, a muffled cry, not quite human, followed by a scratch against the wall.

Elizabeth couldn't take anymore. With one hand out, fingertips trailing the wall, she ran back down the hall toward her room—and yet as she ran she couldn't remember exactly where her room was, or where the door was located. She couldn't remember if there were many doors between her room and the stairs, or even if she'd left her bedroom door open or not.

The terror of not knowing where she was, of whatever was in the stairwell and what might happen next, made her nearly frantic. Her heart was racing, pounding as if it would burst, and she turned in desperate circles. Where was her room? Why had she even left it? And was that thing in the stairs coming toward her?

There was a thump behind her, and then suddenly something brushed her arm. She screamed. She couldn't help it. She was absolutely petrified.

"Elizabeth."

"Kristian." Her voice broke with terror and relief. "Help me. Help me, please."

And he was there, hauling her against him, pulling her into the circle of his arms, his body protecting her. "What is it? What's wrong?"

"There's something out there. There's something…" She could hardly get the words out. Her teeth began chattering and she shivered against him, pressed her face against his cheek, which was hard and broad and smelled even better than it felt. "Scary."

"It's your imagination," he said, his arm firmly around her waist, holding her close.

But the terror still seemed so real, and it was the darkness and her inability to see, to know what it was in the stairwell. If it was human, monster or animal. "There was something. But it's so dark—"

"Is it dark?"

"Yes!" She grabbed at his shirt with both hands. "The lights have been out for ages, and no one came, and they haven't come back on."

"It's the storm. It'll pass."

Her teeth still chattered. "It's too dark. I don't like it."

"Your room is right here," he said, his voice close to her ear. "Come, let's get you bundled up. I'm sure there's a blanket on the foot of the bed."

He led her into her room and found the blanket, draping it around her shoulders. "Better?" he asked.

She nodded, no longer freezing quite as much. "Yes."

"I should go, then."

"No." She reached out, caught his sleeve, and then slid her fingers down to his forearm, which was bare. His skin was warm and taut, covering dense muscle.

For a long silent minute Kristian didn't move, and then he reached out, touched her shoulder, her neck, up to her chin. His fingers ran lightly across her face, tracing her eyebrow, then moving down her nose and across her lips.

"You better send me away," he said gruffly.

She closed her eyes at the slow exploration of his fingertips, her skin hot and growing hotter beneath his touch. "I'll be scared."

"In the morning you'll regret letting me stay."

"Not if I get a good night's sleep."

He rubbed his fingers lightly across her lips, as if learning the curve and shape of her mouth. "If I stay, you won't be sleeping."

She shivered even as nerves twitched to life in her lower back, making her ache and tingle all over. "You shouldn't be so confident."

"Is that a challenge, *latrea mou?*"

He strummed her lower lip, and her mouth quivered. The heat in his skin was making her insides melt and her body crave his. Instinctively her lips parted, to touch and taste his skin.

She heard his quick intake when her tongue brushed his knuckle, and another intake when she slowly drew that knuckle into her mouth. Having his finger in her mouth was doing maddening things to her body, waking a strong physical need that had been slumbering far too long.

She sucked harder on his finger. And the harder she sucked the tighter her nipples peaked and her womb ached. She wanted relief, wanted to be taken, seized, plundered, sated.

"Is this really what you want?" he gritted from between clenched teeth, his deep voice rough with passion.

She didn't speak. Instead she reached toward him, placed her hand on his belt and slowly slid it down to cover his hard shaft.

Kristian groaned deep in his throat and roughly pulled her against him, holding her hips tight against his own. She could feel the surge of heat through his trousers, feel the fabric strain.

Control snapped. He covered her mouth with his and kissed her hard, kissed her fiercely. His lips were firm, demanding, and the pressure of his mouth parted her lips.

She shuddered against him, belly knotting, breasts aching, so that she pressed against him for desperate relief, wanting closer contact with his body, from his thighs to his lean hips to his powerful chest and shoulders. Pressed so closely, she could feel his erection against the apex of her thighs, and as exciting as it felt, it wasn't enough.

She needed him—more of him—more of everything with him. Touch, taste, pressure, skin. "Please," she whispered, circling his waist and slowly running her hands up his back. "Please stay with me."

"For how long?" he murmured, his head dropping to sweep excruciatingly light kisses across the side of her neck and up to the hollow beneath her ear. "Till midnight? Morning? Noon?"

The kisses were making it impossible to think. She pressed her thighs tight, the core of her hot and aching. Years since she'd made love, and now she felt as though she were coming apart here and now.

His mouth found hers again, and the kiss was teasing, light, and yet it made her frantic. She reached up to clasp his head, burying her fingers in his thick glossy hair. "Until as long as you want," she whispered breathlessly.

She'd given him the right answer with her words, and the kiss immediately deepened, his mouth slanting across hers, parting her lips again and drawing her tongue into his mouth. As he sucked on the tip of her tongue she felt her legs nearly buckle. He was stripping her control, seizing her senses, and she was helpless to stop him.

She'd given him a verbal surrender, she thought dizzily, but it wasn't enough. Now he wanted her to surrender her body.

CHAPTER TEN

KRISTIAN felt Elizabeth shiver against him, felt the curve of her hips, the indentation of her waist, the full softness of her breasts.

He'd discovered earlier she was wearing her hair pulled back, with wisps of hair against her face. Kissing her, he now followed one of the wisps to her ear, and he traced that before his fingers slid down the length of her neck.

He could feel her collarbone, and the hollow at her throat, and the thudding of her heart. Her skin was even softer than he remembered, and he found himself fantasizing about taking her hair down, pulling apart the plaits and letting her hair tumble past her shoulders and into his hands.

He wanted her hair, her face, her body in his hands. Wanted her bare and against him.

"Kristian," she said breathlessly, clasping his face in her hands.

Instantly he hardened all over again, his trousers too constricting to accommodate his erection. He wanted out of his clothes. He wanted her out of hers. *Now.*

Elizabeth shuddered as Kristian's hand caressed her hip, down her thigh, to find the hem of her velvet dress. As he lifted the hem she felt air against her bare leg, followed immediately by the heat of his hand.

She let out a slow breath of air, her eyes closing at the path his hand took. His fingers trailed up the outside of her thigh, across her hipbone to the triangle of curls between her legs.

Tensing, shivering, she wanted his touch and yet feared it, too. It had been so long since she'd been held, so long since she'd felt anything as intensely pleasurable as this, that she leaned even closer to him, pressing her breasts to his chest, her tummy to his torso, even as his fingers parted her cleft, finding the most delicate skin between. She was hot, and wet, and she pressed her forehead to his jaw as his fingers explored her.

She couldn't help the moan that escaped her lips, nor the trembling of her legs. She wanted him, needed him, and the intensity of her desire stunned her.

Flushed, dazed, Elizabeth pulled back, swayed on her feet. "The bed," she whispered breathlessly, tugging on his shirt. They walked together, reaching the bed in several steps.

As they bumped into the mattress Kristian impatiently stripped her dress over her head. "I want your hair down, too."

Reaching up, she unpinned her hair and pulled the elastics off the plaits. It was hard to pull her hair apart when Kristian was using her own body against her. With her arms up, over her head, he'd taken her breasts in his hands, cupping their fullness and teasing the tightly ruched nipples.

Gasping at the pressure and pleasure, she very nearly couldn't undo her hair. She hadn't worn a bra tonight due to the sheer lace at her bodice, and the feel of his hands on her bare skin was almost too much.

Hair loose, she reached for Kristian's belt, and then the button and zipper of his trousers. Freeing his shaft, she stroked him, amazed by his size all over again.

But Kristian was impatient to have her on the bed beneath him, and, nudging her backward, he sent her toppling down, legs still dangling over the mattress edge. With her knees parted he kissed her inner thigh, and then higher up, against her warm, moist core. He had a deft touch and tongue, and his expertise was almost more than she could bear. Suddenly shy, she wanted him to stop, but he circled her thighs with his arms, held her open for him.

The tip of his tongue flicked across her heated flesh before playing lightly yet insistently against her core. Again and again he stroked her with his tongue and lips, driving her mad with the tension building inside her. She panted as the pressure built, reached for Kristian, but he dodged her hands, and then, arching, hips bucking, she climaxed.

The orgasm was intense, overwhelming. She felt absolutely leveled. And when Kristian finally moved up, over her, she couldn't even speak. Instead she reached for his chest, slid her fingers across the dense muscle protecting his heart, up over his shoulder to pull him down on top of her.

His body was heavy, hard and strong. She welcomed the weight of him, the delicious feel of his body covering hers. Her orgasm had been intense, but what she really wanted—needed— was something more satisfying than just physical satisfaction. She craved him. The feeling of being taken, loved, sated by him.

He entered her slowly, harnessing his strength to ensure he didn't hurt her. Elizabeth held him tightly, awed by the sensation of him filling her. He felt so good against her, felt so good *in* her. She kissed his chest, the base of his throat, before he dipped his head, covering her mouth with his.

As he kissed her, he slowly thrust into her, stretching his body out over hers to withdraw and then thrust again. His chest grazed her breasts, skin and hair rubbing across her sensitive nipples. She squirmed with pleasure and he buried himself deeper inside her.

Elizabeth wrapped her legs around his waist as his hips moved against her. She squeezed her muscles, holding him inside, and the tantalizing friction of their bodies, the warm heated skin coupled with the deep impenetrable darkness, made their lovemaking even more mysterious and erotic.

As Kristian's tempo increased, his thrusts becoming harder, faster, she met each one eagerly, wanting him, as much of him as he would give her.

No one had ever made her feel so physical, so sexual, or so good. It felt natural being with him, and she gave herself over to Kristian, to his skill and passion, as he drove them both to a point of no return where muscles and nerves tightened and the mind shut out everything but wave after wave of pleasure in the most powerful orgasm of her life.

For those seconds she was not herself, not Grace Elizabeth, but bits of sky and stars and the night. She felt thrown from her body into something so much larger, so much more hopeful than her life. It wasn't sex, she thought, her body still shuddering around him, with him. It was possibility.

Afterwards, feeling dazed and nearly boneless, she clung to Kristian and drew a great gulp of air.

Amazing. That had been so amazing. He made her feel beautiful in every way, too. "I love you," she whispered, against his chest. "I do."

Kristian's hand was buried in her hair, fingers twining through the silken strands. His grip tightened, and then eased, and, dropping his head, he kissed her nose, her brow, her eyelid. "My darling English nurse. Overcome by passion."

"I'm not English," she answered with a supremely satisfied yawn, her body relaxing. "I'm American."

He rolled them over so that he was on the mattress and her weight now rested on him. "What?"

"An American."

"You're *American?*" he repeated incredulously, holding her firmly by the hips.

"Yes."

"Well, that explains a lot of things," he said with mock seriousness. "Especially your sensitivity. Americans are so thin-skinned. They take everything personally."

Her hair spilled over both of them, and she made a face at him in the dark. "I think you were the one who was very sensitive in the beginning. And you were attached to your pain meds—"

"Enough about my pain meds. So, tell me, your eyes… blue? Green? Brown?"

She felt a pang, realizing he might never really know what she looked like. She'd accepted it before, but now it seemed worse somehow. "They're blue. And I'm not that tall—just five-four."

"That's it? When you first arrived a couple weeks ago I was certain you were six feet. That you made Nurse Burly—"

"Hurly," she corrected with a muffled laugh.

"Nurse Hurly-Burly seem dainty."

Elizabeth had to stifle another giggle. "You're terrible, Kristian. You know that, don't you?"

"So you and a half-dozen other nurses keep telling me."

Grinning, she snuggled closer. "So you really had no clue that I was raised in New York?"

"None at all." He kissed the base of her throat, and then up by her ear. "So is that where home is?"

"Was. I've lived in London for years now. I'm happy there."

"Are you?"

"Well, I don't actually live in London. I work in Richmond, and my home is in Windsor. It's under an hour's train ride each way, and I like it. I read, take care of paperwork, sort out my day."

He was stroking her hair very slowly, leisurely, just listening to her talk. As she fell silent, he kissed her again. "My eye specialists are in London."

She wished she could see his face. "Are you thinking of scheduling the eye surgery?"

"Toying with the idea."

"Seriously toying…?"

"Yes. Do you think I should try?"

She considered her words carefully before answering. "You're the one that has to live with the consequences," she said, remembering what Pano had said—that Kristian needed to have something to hope for, something to keep him going.

"But maybe it's better to just know." He exhaled heavily, sounding as if the weight of the world rested on his shoulders. "Maybe I should just do it and get it over with."

Elizabeth put her hand to his chest, felt his heart beating against her hand. "The odds…they're not very good, are they?"

"Less than five percent," he answered, his voice devoid of emotion.

Not good odds, she thought, swallowing hard. "You're doing so well right now. You're making such good progress. If the surgery doesn't turn out as you hoped, could you cope with the results?"

He didn't immediately answer. "I don't know," he said at last. "I don't know how I'd feel. But I know this. I miss seeing. I miss my sight."

"I'm sure you do."

"And I'd love to get rid of the cane. I don't like announcing to the world that I can't see. Besides, I'm sure I look foolish, tapping my way around—"

"That's a ridiculous thing to say!" She pulled away, sat up cross-legged. "First of all, the cane doesn't look foolish, and secondly, it's not about appearances, either. Life and love shouldn't be based on looks. It's about kindness, courage, humility, strength." She paused, drew an unsteady breath. "And you have all those qualities in abundance."

With that, power restored, the lights suddenly flickered and came on.

Elizabeth looked down at them, aware that Kristian couldn't see what she could see and that she should have been embarrassed. They were both naked, he stretched out on his back, she sitting cross-legged, with his hand resting on her bare thigh. But instead of being uncomfortable she felt a little thrill. She felt so right with him. She felt like his—body and soul.

"The power's back," she said, gazing at Kristian, soaking up his dark erotic beauty. His black hair, the strong classic features, impossibly long eyelashes and that sensual mouth of his. "We have lights again."

"Am I missing anything?" he drawled lazily, reaching for her and pulling her back on top of him.

As she straddled his hips he caressed the underside of her breast, so that her nipple hardened and peaked. The touch of his hand against her breast was sending sharp darts of feeling throughout her body, making her insides heat, and clench, and begin to crave relief from his body again.

"No," she murmured, eyes closing, lips helplessly parting as he tugged her lower, allowing him to take her nipple into his mouth. His mouth felt hot and wet against the nipple, and she gripped his shoulders as he sucked, unable to stifle her whimper.

Her whimper aroused him further. Elizabeth could feel him grow hard beneath her. And all she could think was that she wanted him—again. Wanted him to take her—hard, fast— take her until she screamed with pleasure.

He must have been thinking the same thing, too, because,

shifting, he lifted her up, positioned her over him and thrust in. She groaned and shivered as he used his hands to help her ride him. She'd tried this position years ago and hadn't liked it, as she hadn't felt anything much but foolish, and yet now the positions and their bodies clicked. Elizabeth's cheeks burned hot, and her skin glowed as they made love again.

She came faster than before, in a cry of fierce pleasure, before collapsing onto his chest, utterly spent.

Her heart hammering, her body damp, she could do nothing but rest and try to catch her breath. "It just keeps getting better," she whispered.

He stroked her hair, and then the length of her back, until his hand rested on her bottom. "I think I've met my match," he said.

She pushed up on her elbow to see his face. "What does that mean?"

He cupped her breast, stroked the puckered aureola with his thumb. "I think you enjoy sex as much as I do."

"With you. You're incredible."

"It takes two to make it incredible." Reaching up, he pulled her head down to his and kissed her deeply, his tongue teasing hers in another sensual seduction.

In the middle of the kiss, her stomach suddenly growled. Elizabeth giggled apologetically against his mouth. "Sorry. Hungry."

"Then let's find our dinner. I'm starving, too."

They dressed in what they'd left strewn about the floor earlier. Elizabeth bent to retrieve their clothes before handing Kristian first his pants and then his shirt. Slipping on her dress, she struggled to comb her hair smooth with her fingers.

"I feel like I'm in high school," she said with a laugh. And then, and only then, it hit her—Cosima.

"My God," she whispered under her breath, blood draining, her body going icy cold. What had she done? What had she just done?

"Elizabeth?"

She pressed her hand to her mouth, stared at him as he struggled to rebutton his shirt. He'd got it wrong.

"What's the matter?" he demanded.

She could only look at him aghast, shocked, sickened.

She'd behaved badly. *Badly.* He wasn't hers. He'd never been hers. All along he'd belonged to another woman....

"Elizabeth?" Kristian's voice crackled with anger. "Are you still here? Or have you left? Talk to me."

He was right. He couldn't see. Couldn't read her face to know what she was thinking or feeling. "What did we just do, Kristian?" *What did I do?*

His hands stilled, the final button forgotten. A look of confusion crossed his features. "You already have...regrets?"

Regrets? She nearly cried. Only because he wasn't hers.

"Do you have someone waiting for you in London?" he asked, his voice suddenly growing stern, his expression hardening, taking on the glacier stillness she realized he used to keep the world at bay.

"No."

"But there is a relationship?"

"No."

Even without sight he seemed to know exactly where he was, he crossed to her, swiftly closing the distance between them. He took her by the shoulders.

She stiffened, fearing his anger, but then he slid his arms around her, held her securely against him. He kissed her cheek, and then her ear, and then nipped playfully at a particularly sensitive nerve in her neck. "What's wrong, *latrea mou?* Why the second thoughts?"

She splayed her fingers against his chest. Her heart thudded ridiculously hard. "As much as I care about you, Kristian, I cannot do this. It was wrong. *Is* wrong. Just a terrible mistake."

His arms fell away. He stepped back. "Is it because of my eyes? Because I can't see and you pity me?"

"No."

"It's something, *latrea mou*. Because one moment you are in my arms and it feels good, it feels calm and real, like a taste of happiness, and now you say it was…terrible." He drew a breath. "A *mistake*." The bitterness in his voice carved her heart in two. "I think I don't know you at all."

Eyes filling with tears, she watched him take another step backward, and then another. "Kristian." She whispered his name. "No, it's not that. Not the way you make it sound. I loved being with you. I wanted to be near you—"

"Then *what?* Is this about Cosima again? Because, God forgive me, but I can't get away from her. Every time I turn around there she is…even in my goddamn bedroom!"

"Kristian."

"*No.* No. None of that *I'm so disappointed in you* garbage. I've had it. I'm sick of it. What is it with you and Cosima? Is it the contract? The fact that she paid you money? Because if it's money, tell me the amount and I'll cut her a check."

"It's not the money. It's…you. You and her."

He laughed, but the sound grated on her ears. "*Cosima?* Cosima—the Devil Incarnate?"

"You're not a couple?"

"A couple? You're out of your mind, *latrea mou*. She's the reason I couldn't get out of bed, couldn't make myself walk, couldn't face life. Why would I ever want to be with a woman who'd been with my brother?"

Her jaw dropped. Her mouth dried. "Your…*brother?*"

Kristian had gone ashen, and the scar on his cheek tightened. "She was Andreas's fiancée. He's dead because she's alive. He's dead because I went to her aid first. I rescued her for him."

Elizabeth shook her head. Her mouth opened, shut. Of course. *Of course.*

Still shaking her head, she replayed her conversations with Cosima over again. Cosima had never said directly that she was in love with Kristian. She said she'd cared deeply for him, and wanted to see him back in Athens, but she never had said that there was more than that. Just that she hoped…

Hoped.

That was all. That was it.

"So, do you still have to go to Paris on Monday? Or was that just an excuse?" Kristian asked tersely, his features so hard they looked chiseled from granite.

"I still have to go," she answered in a low voice.

"And you still have regrets?"

"Kristian—"

"You do, don't you?"

"Kristian, it's not that simple. Not black and white like that."

"So what *is* it like?" Each word sounded like sharp steel coming from his mouth.

"I…" She closed her eyes, tried to imagine how to tell him who she'd been married to, how she'd been vilified, how she'd transformed herself to escape. But no explanation came. The old pain went too deep. The identities were too confusing. Grace Elizabeth Stiles had been beautiful and wealthy, glamorous and privileged, but she'd also been naïve and dependent, too trusting and too easily hurt.

"You *what?*" he demanded, not about to let her off the hook so easily.

"I can't stay in Greece," she whispered. "I can't."

"Is this all because of that Greek *ornio* you met on your holiday?"

"It was more serious than that."

He stilled. "How serious?"

"I married him."

For a long moment he said nothing, and then his lips pulled and his teeth flashed savagely. "So this is how it is."

She took a step toward him. "What does that mean?"

"It means I'm not a man to you. Not one you can trust or respect—"

"That's not true."

"It *is* true." His shoulders tensed. "We spent two weeks together—morning, noon and night. Why didn't you tell me you were married before? Why did you let me believe it was a simple holiday romance, a little Greek fling gone bad?"

"Because I…I…just don't talk about it."

"Why?"

"Because it hurt me. Badly." Her voice raised, tears started to her eyes. "It made me afraid."

"Just like swimming in the deep end of the pool?"

She bit her bottom lip. He sounded so disgusted, she thought. So irritated and impatient.

"You don't trust me," he added, his tone increasingly cold. "And you don't know me if you think I'd make love to one woman while involved with another."

Her heart sank. He was angry—blisteringly angry.

"What kind of man do you think I am?" he thundered. "How immoral and despicable am I?"

"You're not—"

"You thought I was engaged to Cosima."

"I didn't want to think so."

"But you did," he shot back.

"Kristian, please don't. Please don't judge me—"

"Why not? You judged me."

Tears tumbled. "I love you," she whispered.

He shrugged brusquely. "You don't know the meaning of love if you'd go to bed with a man supposedly engaged to another woman."

Elizabeth felt her heart seize up. This couldn't be happening like this, could it? They couldn't be making such a wretched mess of things, could they? "Kristian, I can't explain it, can't find the words right now, but you must know how I feel—how I really feel. You must know why I'm here, and why I even stayed this long."

"The money, maybe?" he mocked savagely, opening the door wider.

"*No.* And there is no money, I'm not taking her money—"

"Conveniently said."

He didn't know. He didn't see. And maybe that was it. He couldn't see how much she loved him, and how much she believed in him, and how she would have done anything, just about anything, to help him. Love him. Make him happy. "Please," she begged, reaching for him.

But there was no reaching him. Not when he put up that wall of his, that huge, thick, impenetrable ice wall of his, that shut him off from everyone else. Instead he shrugged her off and walked down the hall toward the distant stairwell.

His rejection cut deeply. For a moment she could do nothing but watch him walk away, and then she couldn't just let him go—not like that, not over something that was so small.

A misunderstanding.

Pride.

Ego.

None of it was important enough to keep them apart. None

of it mattered if they truly cared for each other. She loved him, and from the way he'd held her, made love to her, she knew he had to have feelings for her—knew there was more to this than just hormones. For Pete's sake, neither of them were teenagers, and both of them had been through enough to know what mattered.

What mattered was loving, and being loved.

What mattered was having someone on your side. Someone who'd stick with you no matter what.

And so she left the safety of her door, the safety of pride and ego, and followed him to the stairs. She was still wiping away tears, but she knew this—she wasn't going to be dismissed, wasn't going to let him get rid of her like that.

She chased after him, trailing down the staircase. Turning the corner of one landing, she started down the next flight of stairs even as a door opened and footsteps crossed the hall below.

"Kristian!" A man said, his voice disturbingly familiar. "We were just told you'd arrived. What a surprise. Welcome home!"

Nico?

Elizabeth froze. Even her heart seemed to still.

"What are *you* doing here?" Kristian asked, his voice taut, low.

"We—my girlfriend and I—live here part-time," Nico answered. "Didn't you know we'd taken a suite? I was sure you'd been told. At least, I know Pano was aware of it. I talked to him on the phone the other day."

"I've been busy," Kristian murmured distractedly.

Legs shaking, Elizabeth shifted her weight and the floorboard squeaked. All heads down below turned to look up at her.

Elizabeth grabbed the banister. This couldn't be happening. Couldn't be.

Nico, catching sight of her, was equally shocked. Staring up at Elizabeth, he laughed incredulously. "Grace?"

Elizabeth could only stare back.

Nico glanced at Kristian, and then back to his ex-wife. "What's going on?" he asked.

"I don't know," Kristian answered tightly. "You tell me."

"I don't know either," Nico said, frowning at Elizabeth. "But for a moment I thought you and Grace were…together."

"Grace who?" Kristian demanded tersely.

"Stile. My American wife."

Kristian went rigid. "There's no Grace here."

"Yes, there she is," Nico answered. "She's standing on the landing. Blonde hair. Black lace dress."

Elizabeth felt Kristian's confusion as he swung around, staring blindly up at the stairwell. Her heart contracted. "Kristian," she said softly, hating his confusion, hating that she was the source of it, too.

"That's not Grace," Kristian retorted grimly. "That's Elizabeth. Elizabeth Hatchet. My nurse."

"Nurse?" Nico laughed. "Oh, dear, Koumantaros, it looks like she's duped you. Because your Elizabeth is my ex-wife, Grace Stile. And a nasty gold-digger, too."

CHAPTER ELEVEN

KRISTIAN felt as though he'd been punched hard in the gut. He couldn't breathe, couldn't move, could only stand there, struggling to take in air.

Elizabeth wasn't Elizabeth? Elizabeth was really Grace Stile?

He tried to shake his head, tried to clear the fuzz and storm clouding his mind.

The woman he'd fallen in love with wasn't even who he thought she was. Her name wasn't even Elizabeth. Maybe she wasn't even a nurse.

Maybe she was a gold-digger, just like Nico said.

Gold-digger. The word rang in Elizabeth's head.

Shocked, she went hot, and then cold, and hot again. "I'm no gold-digger," she choked, finally finding her voice. Legs wobbling, she took one step and then another until she'd reached the hall. "*You* are," she choked. "You, you… you're…" But she couldn't get the words out, couldn't defend herself, could scarcely breathe, much less think.

Nico had betrayed *her.*

Nico had married *her* for her money.

Nico had poisoned the Greek media and public against her.

Stomach roiling, she was swept back into that short brutal marriage and the months following their divorce.

He'd made her life a living hell and she'd been the one to pay—and pay, and pay. Not just for the divorce, and not just his settlement, but emotionally, physically, mentally. It had taken years to heal, years to stop being so hurt and so insecure and so angry. *Angry.*

And she had been angry because she'd felt cheated of love, cheated of the home and the family and the dreams she'd cherished. They were supposed to have been husband and wife. A couple, partners.

But she'd only been money, cash, the fortune to supplement Nico's dwindling inheritance.

Nico, though, wasn't paying her the least bit of attention. He was still talking to Kristian, a smirk on his face—a face she'd once thought so handsome. She didn't find him attractive anymore, not even if she was being objective, because, next to Kristian, Nico's good-looks faded to merely boyish, almost pretty, whereas Kristian was fiercely rugged, all man.

"She'll seduce you," Nico continued, rolling back on his heels, his arms crossed over his chest. "And make you think it was your idea. And when she has you in bed she'll tell you she loves you. She'll make you think it's love, but it's greed. She'll take you for everything you're worth—"

"That's enough. I've heard enough," Kristian ground out, silencing Nico's ruthless character assassination. He'd paled, so that the scar seemed to jump from his cheekbone, a livid reminder of the tragedy that had taken so much from him over a year ago.

"None of it is true," Elizabeth choked, her body shaking, legs like jelly. "Nothing he says—"

"I said, *enough.*" Kristian turned away and walked down the hall.

Elizabeth felt the air leave her, her chest so empty her heart seized.

Somehow she found her way back to her room and stumbled into bed, where she lay stiff as a board, unable to sleep or cry.

Everything seemed just so unbelievably bad—so awful that it couldn't even be assimilated.

Lying there, teeth chattering with shock and cold, Elizabeth prayed that when the sun finally rose in the morning all of this would be just a bad, bad dream.

It wasn't.

The next morning a maid knocked on Elizabeth's door, giving her the message that a car was ready to drive her to meet the helicopter.

Washing her face, Elizabeth avoided looking at herself in the mirror before smoothing the wrinkles in her velvet dress and heading downstairs, where the butler ushered her to the waiting car.

Elizabeth had been under the impression that she'd be traveling back alone, but Kristian was already in the car when she climbed in.

"Good morning," she whispered, sliding onto the seat but being careful to keep as much distance between them as she could.

His head barely inclined.

She ducked her head, stared at her fingers, which were laced and locked in her lap. Sick, she thought, so sick. She felt as though everything good and warm and hopeful inside her had vanished, left, gone. Died.

Eyes closing, she held her breath, her teeth sinking into her lower lip.

She only let her breath out once the car started moving, leaving the castle for the helicopter pad on the other side of town.

"You were Nico's wife," Kristian said shortly, his deep rough voice splitting the car's silence in two. There was a brutality in his voice she'd never heard before. A violence that spoke of revenge and embittered passion.

Opening her eyes, she looked at Kristian, but she couldn't read anything in his face—not when his fiercely handsome features were so frozen, fixed in hard, remote, unforgiving lines. It was as if his face wasn't a face but a mask.

The car seemed to spin.

She didn't answer, didn't want to answer, didn't know *how* to answer—because in his present frame of mind nothing she said would help, nothing she said would matter. After all, Kristian Koumantaros was a Greek man. It wouldn't matter to him that she was divorced—had been divorced for years. In his mind she'd always be Nico's wife.

Elizabeth glanced down at her hands again, the knuckles white. She was so dizzy she didn't think she could sit straight, but finally she forced her head up, forced the world's wild revolutions to slow until she could see Kristian on the seat next to her, his blue eyes brilliant, piercing, despite the fact that she knew he couldn't see.

"I'm waiting," he said flatly, finality and closure in his rough voice.

Tears filling her eyes, she drew another deep breath. "Yes," she said, her voice so faint it sounded like nothing.

"So your name isn't really Elizabeth, is it?"

Again she couldn't speak. The pain inside her chest was excruciating. She could only stare at Kristian, wishing everything had somehow turned out differently. If Nico hadn't been one of the castle's tenants. If Cosima hadn't stood between them. If Elizabeth had understood just who and what Cosima really was…

"I'm still waiting," Kristian said.

Hurt and pain flared, lighting bits of fire inside her. "Waiting for what?" she demanded, shoulders twisted so she could better see him. "For some big confession? Well, I'm not going to confess. I've done nothing wrong—"

"You've done *everything* wrong," he interrupted through gritted teeth. "Everything. If your name isn't really Elizabeth Hatchet."

Colder and colder, she swallowed, her eyes growing wide, her stomach plummeting.

"If Nico was your husband, that makes you someone I do not know."

Elizabeth exhaled so hard it hurt, her chest spasming, her throat squeezing closed.

When she didn't answer, he leaned toward her, touched the side of her head, then her ear and finally her cheekbones, her eyes, her nose, her mouth. "You are Grace Stile, aren't you?"

"Was," she barely whispered. "I was Grace Stile. But Grace Stile doesn't exist anymore."

"Grace Stile was a beautiful woman," he said mockingly, his fingertips lingering on the fullness of her soft mouth.

She trembled inwardly at the touch. "I am not her," she said against his fingers. Last night he'd made her feel so good, so warm, so safe. *Happy.* But today…today it was something altogether different.

He ground out a mocking laugh. "Grace Stile, daughter of an American icon—"

"No."

"New York's most beautiful and accomplished debutante."

"Not me."

"Even more wealthy than the Greek tycoon she married."
Elizabeth stopped talking.

"Your father, Rupert Stile—"

She pulled her head away, leaned back in her seat to
remove herself from his touch. "Grace Stile is gone," she said
crisply. "I am Elizabeth Hatchet, a nursing administrator, and
that is all that is important, all that needs to be known."

He barked a laugh, far from amused. "But your legal name
isn't even Elizabeth Hatchet."

She hesitated, bit savagely into her lower lip, knowing
she'd never given anyone this information—not since that
fateful day when everything had changed. "Hatchet was my
mother's maiden name. Legally I'm Grace Elizabeth."

He laughed again, the sound even more strained and in-
credulous. "Are you even a registered nurse?"

"Of course!"

"Of course," he repeated, shaking his head and running a hand
across his jaw, which was dark with a day's growth of beard.

For a moment neither spoke, and the only sound was
Kristian's palm, rubbing the rough bristles on his chin and jaw.

"You think you know someone," he said, after a tense
minute. "You think you know what's true, what's real, and
then you find out you know nothing at all."

"But you do know I am a nurse," she said steadfastly. "And
I hold a Masters Degree in Business Administration."

"But I don't know that. I can't see. You could be just
anybody…and it turns out you are!"

"Kristian—"

"Because if I weren't blind you couldn't have pulled this off,
could you? If I could see I would have recognized you. I would
have known you weren't some dreary, dumpy little nursing administrator, but the famously beautiful heiress Grace Stile."

"That never crossed my mind—"

"No? Are you sure?"

"Yes."

He made a rough, derogatory sound. His mouth slanted, cheekbones pronounced. The car had stopped. They were at the small airport, and not far from their car waited the helicopter and pilot. As the driver of the car turned off the ignition, Kristian laid a hand on Elizabeth's thigh.

"Your degrees," he said. "Those are in which name?"

She felt the heat of his hand sear her skin even as it melted her on the inside. She cared for him, loved him, but couldn't seem to connect anything that was happening today with what had taken place in her bed last night.

"My degrees," she said softly, referring to her nursing degree and then the degree in Business Administration, "were both earned in England, as Elizabeth Hatchet."

"Very clever of you," he taunted, as the passenger door opened and the driver stood there, ready to provide assistance.

Elizabeth suppressed a wave of panic. It was all coming to an end, so quickly and so badly, and she couldn't figure out how to turn the tide now that it was rushing at her, fierce and relentless.

"Kristian," she said urgently, touching his hand, her fingers attempting to slide around his. But he held his fingers stiff, and aloof, as though they'd never been close. "There was nothing clever about it. I moved to England and changed my name, out of desperation. I didn't want to be Grace Stile anymore. I wanted to start over. I *needed* to start over. And so I did."

He didn't speak again. Not even after they were in the helicopter heading for Athens, where he'd told her a plane awaited. He was sending her home immediately. Her bags were already at Athens airport. She'd be back in London by mid-afternoon.

It was a strangely silent flight, and it wasn't until they were on the ground in Athens, exiting the helicopter, that he broke the painful stillness.

"Why medicine?" he demanded.

Kristian's question stopped her just as she was about to climb the private jet's stairs.

Slowly she turned to face him, tucking a strand of hair behind her ear even as she marveled all over again at the changes two weeks had made. Kristian Koumantaros was every inch the formidable tycoon he'd been before he was injured. He wasn't just walking, he stood tall, legs spread, powerful shoulders braced.

"You didn't study medicine at Smith or Brown or wherever you went in the States," he continued, naming universities on the East Coast. "You were interested in antiquities then."

Antiquities, she thought, her teeth pressed to the inside of her lower lip. She and her love of ancient cultures. Wasn't that how she'd met Nico in the first place? Attending a party at a prestigious New York museum to celebrate the opening of a new, priceless Greek exhibit?

"Medicine's more practical," she answered, eyes gritty, stinging with tears she wouldn't let herself cry.

And, thinking back to her move across the Atlantic, to her new identity and her new choices, she knew she'd been compelled to become someone different, someone better…more altruistic.

"Medicine is also about helping others—doing something good."

"Versus exploiting their weaknesses?"

"I've never done that!" she protested hotly.

"No?"

"No." But she could see from his expression that he didn't

believe her. She opened her mouth to defend herself yet again, before stopping. It didn't matter, she thought wearily, pushing another strand of hair back from her face. He would think what he wanted to think.

And, fine, let him.

She cared about him—hugely, tremendously—but she was tired of being the bad person, was unwilling to be vilified any longer. She'd never been a bad woman, a bad person. Maybe at twenty-three, or twenty-four she hadn't known better than to accept the blame, but she did now. She was a woman, not a punching bag.

"Goodbye," she said *"Kali tihi."* Good luck.

"Good luck?" he repeated. "With what?" he snapped, taking a threatening step toward her.

His reaction puzzled her. But he'd always puzzled her. "With everything," she answered, just wanting to go now, needing to make the break. She knew this could go nowhere. Last night she should have realized that nothing good would come out of an inappropriate liaison, but last night she hadn't been thinking. Last night she'd been frightened and uncertain, and she'd turned to him for comfort, turned to him for reassurance. It was the worst thing she could have done.

And yet Kristian still marched toward her, his expression black. "And just what is *everything?*"

She thought of all he had still waiting for him. He could have such a good life, such a rich, interesting life—sight or no sight—if he wanted.

Her lips curved in a faint, bittersweet smile. "Your life," she said simply. "It's all still before you."

And quickly, before he could detain her, she climbed the stairs, disappearing into the jet's cool, elegant interior where she settled into one of the leather chairs in the main cabin.

Except for the flight crew, the plane was empty.

Elizabeth fastened her seatbelt and settled back in the club chair. She knew it would be a very quiet trip home.

Back in London, Elizabeth rather rejoiced in the staggering number of cases piled high on her desk. She welcomed the billing issues, the cranky patients, the nurses needing vacations and personal days off, as every extra hour of work meant another hour she couldn't think about Kristian, or Greece, or the chaotic two weeks spent there.

Because now that she was back in England, taking the train to work at her office in Richmond every day, she couldn't fathom what had happened.

Couldn't fathom how it had happened.

Couldn't fathom why.

She wasn't interested in men, or dating, or having another lover. She wasn't interested in having a family, either. All she wanted was to work, to pay her bills, to keep her company running as smoothly as possible. Her business was her professional life, social life and personal life all rolled into one, and it suited her just fine.

Far better to be Plain Jane than Glamorous Grace Stile, with the world at her feet, because the whole world-at-your-feet thing was just an illusion anyway. As she'd learned the hard way, the more people thought you had, the more they envied you, and then resented you, and eventually they lobbied to see you fall.

Far better to live simply and quietly and mind your own business, she thought, shuffling papers into her briefcase.

She was leaving work early again today, tormented by a stomach bug that wouldn't go away. She'd been back home in England just over two months now, but she hadn't felt like herself for ages. Since Greece, as a matter of fact.

Her secretary glanced up as Elizabeth opened the office door.

"Still under the weather, Ms. Hatchet?" Mrs. Shipley asked sympathetically, pushing her reading glasses up on her head.

Mrs. Shipley had practically run the office single-handedly while Elizabeth was gone, and she couldn't imagine a better administrative assistant.

"I am," Elizabeth answered with a grimace, as her insides did another sickly, queasy rise and fall that made her want to throw up into the nearest rubbish bin. But of course she never had the pleasure of actually throwing up. She wasn't lucky enough to get the thing—whatever it was—out of her system.

"If you picked up a parasite in Greece, you'll need a good antibiotic, my dear. I know I'm sounding like a broken record, but you really should see a doctor. Get something for that. The right antibiotic will nip it in the bud. And you need it nipped in the bud, as you look downright peaky."

Mrs. Shipley was right. Elizabeth felt absolutely wretched. She ached. Her head throbbed. Her stomach alternated between nausea and cramps. Even her sleep was disturbed, colored with weird, wild dreams of doom and gloom.

But what she feared most, and refused to confront, was the very real possibility that it wasn't a parasite she'd picked up but something more permanent. Something more changing.

Something far more serious.

Like Kristian Koumantaros's baby.

She'd been home just over two months now and she hadn't had her period—which wasn't altogether unusual, since she was the least regular woman she knew—but she couldn't bring herself to actually take a pregnancy test.

If she wasn't pregnant—fantastic.

If she was…

If she was?

The next morning her nausea was so severe she huddled next to the toilet, managing nothing more than wrenching dry heaves.

Her head was spinning and she was gagging, and all she could think was, What if I really am pregnant with Kristian Koumantaros's baby?

Kristian Koumantaros was one of the most wealthy, powerful, successful men in Europe. He lived in ancient monasteries and castles and villas all over the world. He traveled by helicopter, private jet, luxury yacht. He negotiated with no one.

And she knew he wouldn't negotiate with her. If he knew she was pregnant he'd step in, take over, take action.

And, yes, Kristian *ought* to know. But how would he benefit from knowing? Would the baby—if there really was a baby—benefit?

Would *she?*

No. Not when Kristian viewed her as a heartless mercenary, a gold-digger, someone who preyed upon other's weaknesses.

Elizabeth somehow managed to drag herself into work, drag listlessly through the day, and then caught the train home to Windsor.

Sitting on the train seat, thirty minutes away from her stop, it hit her for the first time. She was pregnant. She knew deep down she was going to have a baby.

But Kristian. What about Kristian?

A wave of ice flooded her. What would he say, much less do, if he knew about the baby? He didn't even like her. He despised her. How would he react if he knew she carried his child?

Panic flooded her—panic that made her feel even colder and more afraid.

She couldn't let him find out. She wouldn't let him find out.

Stop it, she silently chastised herself as her panic grew. It's not as though you'll bump into him.

You live on opposite ends of the continent. You're both on islands separated by seas. No way to accidentally meet.

As heartless as it sounded, she'd make sure they wouldn't meet, either.

He'd take the baby. She knew he'd take the baby from her. Just the way Nico had taken everything from her.

Greek men were proud, and fierce. Greek men, particularly Greek tycoons, thought they were above rules and laws. And Kristian Koumantaros, now that he was nearly recovered, would be no different.

Elizabeth's nausea increased, and she stirred restlessly in her seat, anxious to be home, where she could take a long bath, climb into bed and just relax.

She needed to relax. Her heart was pounding far too hard.

Trying to distract herself, she glanced around the train cabin, studying the different commuters, before glancing at the man next to her reading a newspaper. His face was hidden by the back of the paper and her gaze fell on the headlines. Nothing looked particularly interesting until she read, *Koumantaros in London for Treatment.*

Koumantaros.

Kristian Koumantaros?

Breath catching, she leaned forward to better see the article. She only got the first line or two before the man rudely shuffled the pages and turned his back to her preventing her from reading more.

But Elizabeth didn't need to read much more than those first two lines to get the gist of the article.

Kristian had undergone the risky eye surgery at Moorfield's Hospital in London today.

CHAPTER TWELVE

WALKING from the train station to her little house, Elizabeth felt her nerves started getting the best of her. For the past three years she'd made historic Windsor her home, having found it the perfect antidote to the stresses of her career, but today the walk filled her with apprehension.

Something felt wrong. And it wasn't just thinking about the baby. It was an uneasy sixth sense that things around her weren't right.

Picking up her pace, she tried to silence her fears, telling herself she was tired and overly imaginative.

No one was watching her.

No one was following her.

And nothing bad was going to happen.

But tugging the collar of her coat up, and crossing her arms over her chest to keep warm, she couldn't help thinking that something felt bad. And the bad feeling was growing stronger as she left the road and hurried up the crushed gravel path toward her house.

Windsor provided plenty of diversion on weekends, with brilliant shopping as well as the gorgeous castle and the river-side walks, but as she entered her house and closed the door behind her, her quiet little house on its quiet little lane seemed very isolated.

If someone had followed her home, no one would see.

If someone broke into her house, no one would hear her cries for help.

Elizabeth locked the front door, then went through the kitchen to the back door, checking the lock on that before finally taking her coat off and turning the heat up.

In the kitchen she put on the kettle for tea, and was just about to make some toast when a knock sounded on her door.

She froze, the loaf of bread still in her hands, and stood still so long that the knock sounded again.

Putting the bread on the counter, and the knife down, she headed for the door, checking through a window first before she actually opened it.

A new model Jaguar was parked out front, and a man stood on her doorstep, his back to her as he faced the car. But she knew the man—knew his height, the breadth of his shoulders, the length of his legs, the shape of his head.

Kristian.

Kristian here.

But today was his surgery…he was supposed to have had surgery…the paper had said…

Unless he'd backed out.

But he wouldn't back out, would he?

Heart hammering, she undid the lock and opened the door, and the sound of the lock turning caught his attention. Kristian shifted, turning toward her. But as he faced her his eyes never blinked, and his expression remained impassive.

"Kristian," she whispered, cold all over again.

"Cratchett," he answered soberly.

And looking up into his face, a face so sculpturally perfect, the striking features contrasted by black hair and blue eyes, she thought him a beautiful but fearsome angel. One sent to judge her, punish her.

Glancing past him to the car, the sleek black Jaguar with tinted windows, she wondered how many cars he had scattered all over the world.

"You're…here," she said foolishly, her mind so strangely blank that nothing came to her—nothing but shock and fear. He couldn't know. He didn't know. She'd only found out today herself.

"Yes, I am." His head tipped and he looked at her directly, but still without recognition. She felt her heart turn over with sympathy for him. He hadn't gone through with the surgery. He must have had second thoughts. And while she didn't blame him—it was a very new, very dangerous procedure—it just reaffirmed all over again her determination to keep the pregnancy a secret…at least for now.

"How did you know I lived here?"

"I had your address," he said blandly.

"Oh. I see." But she didn't see. Her home address was on nothing—although she supposed if a man like Kristian Koumantaros wanted to know where she lived it wouldn't take much effort on his part to find out. He had money, and connections. People would tell him things, particularly private detectives—not that he'd do that…

Or would he?

Frowning, bewildered, she stared up at him, still trying to figure out what he was doing here in Windsor—on her doorstep, no less.

From the kitchen, her kettle began to whistle.

His head lifted, his black brows pulling.

"The kettle," she said, by way of explanation. "I was just

making tea. I should turn it off." And without waiting for him to answer she went to the kitchen and unplugged the kettle, only to turn around and discover Kristian right there behind her, making her small, old-fashioned kitchen, with its porcelain farm sink and simple farmhouse table, look tired and primitive.

"Oh," she said, taking a nervous step back. "You're here."

The corner of his mouth twisted. "I appear to be everywhere today."

"Yes." She pressed her skirt smooth, her hands uncomfortably damp. How had he made his way into the kitchen so quickly? It was almost as if he knew his way already—or as if he could actually see…

Could he?

Her pulse quickened, her nerves strung so tight she felt disturbingly close to falling apart. It had been such an overwhelming day as it was. First her certainty about the baby, and now Kristian in her house.

"Have you been in England long?" she asked softly, trying to figure out just what was going on.

"I've spent part of the last month here."

A month in England. Her heart jumped a little, and she had to exhale slowly to try to calm herself. "I didn't know."

One of his black eyebrows lifted, but he said nothing else. At least some things hadn't changed, she thought. He was still as uncommunicative as ever. But that didn't mean she had to play his game.

"The surgery—it was scheduled for today, wasn't it?" she asked awkwardly.

"Why?"

"I read it in the paper…actually, it was on the train home. You were supposed to have the treatment done today in London."

"Really?"

She felt increasingly puzzled. "It's what the paper said," she repeated defensively."

"I see." He smiled benignly. And the conversation staggered to a stop there.

Uncertainly, she turned to pour her tea.

Good manners required her to ask if he'd like a cup, but the last thing she wanted to do was prolong this miserable visit.

She wrestled with her conscience. Good manners won. "Would you like some tea?" she asked, voice stilted.

White teeth flashed in a mocking smile. "I thought you'd never ask."

Hands shaking, she retrieved another cup and saucer from the cupboard before filling his cup.

He couldn't see…could he?

He couldn't possibly see…

But something inside her, that same peculiar sixth sense from earlier, made her suspicious.

"Toast?" Her voice quavered. She hated that. She hated that suddenly everything felt so wildly out of control.

"No, thank you."

Glancing at him, she put the bread away, too nervous now to eat.

"You're not going to eat?" he asked mildly.

"No."

"You're not hungry?"

Her stomach did another uncomfortable freefall. How did he know she wasn't going to eat?

"The surgery," she said. "You didn't have it today."

"No." He paused for the briefest moment. "I had it a month ago."

Her legs nearly went from beneath her. Elizabeth put a

hand out to the kitchen table to support herself. "A month ago?" she whispered, her gaze riveted to his face.

"Mmmm."

He wasn't helping at all, was he? She swallowed around the huge lump filling her throat. "Can you, can you…see?"

"Imperfectly."

Imperfectly, she repeated silently, growing increasingly light-headed. "Tell me…tell me…how much do you see?"

"It's not all dark anymore. One eye is more or less just shadows and dark shapes, but with the other eye I get a bit more. While I'll probably never be able to drive or pilot my own plane again, I can see you."

"And what do you see…now?" Her voice was faint to her own ears.

"You."

Her heart was beating so hard she was afraid she'd faint.

"The colors aren't what they were," he added. "Everything's faded, so the world's rather gray and white, but I know you're standing near a table. You're touching the table with one hand. Your other hand is on your stomach."

He was right. He was exactly right. And her hand was on her stomach because she felt like throwing up. "Kristian."

He just looked at her, really looked at her, and she didn't know whether to smile for him or burst into tears. He could see. Imperfectly, as he'd said, but something was better than nothing. Something meant he'd live independently more easily. He'd also have more power in his life again, as well as control.

Control.

And suddenly she realized that if he could see her, he'd eventually see the changes in her body. He'd know she was pregnant…

Her insides churned.

"Is that why you're here tonight?" she asked. "To tell me your good news?"

"And to celebrate your good news."

She swayed on her feet. "My good news?"

"You do have good news, don't you?" he persisted.

Elizabeth stared at Kristian where he stood, just inside the kitchen doorway. Protectively she rubbed her stomach, over her not yet existent bump, trying to stay calm. "I…I don't think so."

"I suppose it depends on how you look at it," he answered. His mouth slanted, black lashes lowering to conceal the startling blue of his eyes. "We knew each other only two weeks and two days, and that was two months and two weeks ago. Those two weeks were mostly good. But there was a disappointment or two, wasn't there?"

She couldn't tear her eyes off him. He looked strong and dynamic, and his tone was commanding. "A couple," she echoed nervously.

"One of the greatest offenses is that we flew to Kithira for dinner and we never ate. We were in my favorite restaurant and we never enjoyed an actual meal."

Elizabeth crossed her arms over her chest. "That's your *greatest* disappointment?"

"If you'd ever eaten there, you'd understand. It's truly great food. Greek food as it's meant to be."

She blinked, her fingers balling into knuckled fists. "You're here to tell me I missed out on a great meal?"

"It was supposed to be a special evening."

He infuriated her. Absolutely infuriated her. Pressing her fists to her ribs, she shook inwardly with rage. Here she was, exhausted from work, stressed and sick from her pregnancy, worried about his sight, deeply concerned about the future, and all he could think of was a missed meal?

"Why don't you have your pilot take you back to Kithira and you can *have* your delicious dinner?" she snapped.

"But that wouldn't help you. You still wouldn't know what a delicious meal you'd missed." He gestured behind him, to the compact living room. "So I've brought that meal to you."

"What?"

"I won't have you flying in your state, and I'm worrying about the baby."

"What baby?" she choked, her veins filling with a flood of ice water.

"Our baby," he answered simply, turning away and heading for the living room, which had been transformed while they were in the kitchen.

The owner of the Kithirian restaurant, along with the waiter who had served them that night, had set up a table, chairs, covering the table in a crisp white cloth and table settings for two. The lights had been turned down and candles flickered on the table, and on the side table next to her small antique sofa, and somewhere, she didn't know where, music played.

They'd turned her living room into a Greek taverna and Elizabeth stood rooted to the spot, unable to take it all in. "What's going on?"

Kristian shrugged. "We're going to have that dinner tonight. Now." He moved to take one of the chairs, and pulled it out for her. "A Greek baby needs Greek food."

"Kristian—"

"It's true." His voice dropped, and his expression hardened. "You're having our baby."

"My baby."

"Our baby," he corrected firmly. "And it is *our* baby." His blue gaze held hers. "Isn't it?"

With candles flickering on the crisp white cloth, soft Greek music in the background, and darkly handsome Kristian here before her, Elizabeth felt tears start to her eyes. Two months without a word from him. Two months without apology, remorse, forgiveness. Two months of painful silence and now this—this power-play in her living room.

"I know you haven't been feeling well," he continued quietly. "I know because I've been in London, watching over you."

Weakly she sat down—not at the table, but on one of her living room chairs. "You think I'm a gold-digger."

"A gold-digger? Grace Stile? A woman as wealthy as Athina Onassis Roussel?"

Elizabeth clasped her hands in her lap. "I don't want to talk about Grace Stile."

"I do." He dropped into a chair opposite her. "And I want to talk about Nico and Cosima and all these other sordid characters appearing in our own little Greek play."

The waiter and the restaurant owner had disappeared into the kitchen. They must have begun warming or preparing food, as the smell coming from the back of the house made her stomach growl.

"I know Nico put you through hell in your marriage," Kristian continued. "I know the divorce was even worse. He drove you out of Greece and the media hounded you for years after. I don't blame you for changing your name, for moving to England and trying to become someone else."

She held her breath, knowing there was a *but* coming. She could hear it in his voice, see it in the set of his shoulders.

"But," he added, "I minded very much not being able to see you. Much more not being able to see—and assess—the situation that night at the Kithira castle for myself."

She linked her fingers to hide the fact they were trembling.

"That evening was a nightmare. I just want to forget it. Forget them. Forget Grace, too."

"I can't forget Grace." His head lifted and his gaze searched her face. "Because she's beautiful. And she's you."

The lump in her throat burned, swelled, making everything inside her hurt worse. "I'm not beautiful."

"You were beautiful as a New York debutante, and you're even more beautiful now. And it has nothing to do with your name, or the Stile fortune. Nothing to do with your marriage or your divorce or the work you do as an administrator. It's you. Grace Elizabeth."

"You don't know me," she whispered, trying to silence him.

"But I do. Because for two weeks I lived with you and worked with you and dined with you, and you changed me. You saved me—"

"No."

"Elizabeth, I didn't want to live after the accident. I didn't want to feel so much loss and pain. But you somehow gave me a window of light, and hope. You made me believe that things could be different. Better."

"I wasn't that good, or nice."

"No, you weren't nice. But you were strong. Tough. And you wouldn't baby me. You wouldn't allow me to give up. And I needed that. I needed you." He paused. "I still do."

Her eyes closed. Hot tears stung her eyelids.

He reached over, skimmed her cheeks with his fingers. "Don't cry," he murmured. "Please don't cry."

She shook her head, then turned her cheek into his palm, biting her lip to keep the tears from falling. "If you needed me, why did you let me go?"

"Because I didn't feel worthy of you. Didn't feel like a man who deserved you."

"Kristian—"

"I realized that night that if I'd been able to see, I would have been in control at the castle in Kithira. I could have read the situation, understood what was happening. Instead I stood there in the dark   literally, figuratively—and it enraged me. I felt trapped. Helpless. My blindness was creating ignorance. Fear."

"You've never been scared of anything," she protested softly.

"Since the accident I've been afraid of everything. I've been haunted by nightmares, my sleep disturbed until I thought I was going mad, but after meeting you that began to change. I began to change. I began to find my way home—my way back to me."

She simply stared at him, her heart tender, her eyes stinging from unshed tears.

"I am a man who takes care of his woman," he continued quietly. "I hated not being able to take care of you. And you are my woman. You've been mine from the moment you arrived in the Taygetos on that ridiculous donkey cart."

Her lips quivered in a tremulous smile. "That was the longest, most uncomfortable ride of my life."

"Elizabeth, *latrea mou,* I have loved you from the very first day I met you. You were horrible and wonderful and your courage won me over. Your courage and your compassion. Your kindness and your strength. All those virtues you talked about in Kithira. You told me appearances didn't matter. You said there were virtues far more important and I agree. Yes, you're beautiful, but I couldn't see your beauty until today. I didn't need your beauty, or the Stile name, or your inheritance to win me. I just needed you. With me."

"Kristian—"

"I still do."

Eyes filmed by tears, she looked up, around her small living room. Normally it was a rather austere room. She lived off her salary, having donated nearly all of her inheritance to charity, and it never crossed her mind to spoil herself with pretty things. But tonight the living room glowed, cozy and intimate with candlelight, the beautifully set table and strains of Greek music, even as the most delectable smells wafted from the kitchen.

The restaurant owner appeared in the doorway. "Dinner is ready," he said sternly. "And tonight you both must eat."

Elizabeth joined Kristian at the table, and for the first time in weeks she enjoyed food. How could she not enjoy the meal tonight? Everything was wonderful. The courses and flavors were beyond brilliant. They shared marinated lamb, fish with tomatoes and currants, grilled octopus—which Elizabeth did pass on—and as she ate she couldn't look away from Kristian.

She'd missed him more than she knew.

Just having him here, with her, made everything feel right. Made everything feel good. Intellectually she knew there were problems, issues, and yet emotionally she felt calm and happy and peaceful again.

It had always been like this with him. It wasn't what he said, or did. It was just him. He made her feel good. He made her feel wonderful.

Looking across the table at him, she felt a thought pop into her head. "You know, Cosima said—" she started to say, before breaking off. She'd done it again. Cosima. Always Cosima. "Why do I keep talking about her?"

"I don't know. But you might as well tell me what she said. I might as well hear all of it."

"It's nothing—not important. Let's forget it."

"No. You brought it up, so it's obviously on your mind. What did Cosima say?"

Elizabeth silently kicked herself. The dinner had been

going so well. And now she'd done the same thing as at the castle in Kithira. Her nose wrinkled. "I'm sorry, Kristian."

"So tell me. What does she say?"

"That before you were injured you were an outrageous playboy." She looked up at him from beneath her eyelashes. "That you could get any woman to eat out of your hand. I was just thinking that I can see what she meant."

Kristian coughed, a hint of color darkening his cheekbones. "I've never been a playboy."

"Apparently women can't resist you…ever."

He gave her a pointed look. "That's not true."

"So you didn't have two dates, on two different continents, in the same day?"

"Geographically as well as physically impossible."

"Unless you were flying from Sydney to Los Angeles."

Kristian grimaced. "That was a one-time situation. If it hadn't been for crossing the time zones it wouldn't have been the same day."

Elizabeth smiled faintly, rather liking Kristian in the hot seat. "Do you miss the lifestyle?"

"No—God, no." Now it was his turn to smile, his white teeth flashing against the bronze of his skin. Sun and exercise had given him the most extraordinary golden glow. "Being a playboy isn't a picnic," he intoned mockingly. "Some men envied the number of relationships I had, but it was really quite demanding, trying to keep all the women happy."

She was amused despite herself. "You're shameless."

"Not as shameless as you were last August, checking me out by the pool…*despite* us having a deal."

"I *wasn't* looking."

"You were. Admit it."

She blushed. "You couldn't even see."

"I could tell. Some things one doesn't need to see to know. Just as I didn't need to see you to know I love you. That I will always love you. And I want nothing more than to spend the rest of my life with you."

Elizabeth's breath caught in her throat. She couldn't speak. She couldn't even breathe.

Kristian stood up from the table and crossed around to kneel before her. He had a ring box in his hand. "Marry me, *latrea mou*," he said. "Marry me. Come live with me. I don't want to live without you."

His proposal shocked her, and frightened her. It wasn't that she didn't care for him—she did, oh, she did—but *marriage*. Marriage to another Greek tycoon.

She drew back in her chair. "Kristian, I can't... I'm sorry, I can't."

"You don't want to be with me?"

All she wanted was to be with him, but marriage terrified her. To her it represented an abuse of power and control, and she never wanted to feel trapped like that again.

"I do want to be with you—but marriage..." Her voice cracked. She felt the old pressure return, the sense of dread and futility. "Kristian, I just had such a terrible time of it. And it shattered me when it ended. I can't go that route again."

"You can," he said, rising.

"No, I can't. I really can't." She slid off her chair and left the table. She felt cornered now, and she didn't know where to go. He was in her house. The restaurant owner and the waiter were in her house. And it was a little two-bedroom house.

Elizabeth retreated to the only other room—her bedroom—but Kristian followed. He put his hand out to keep her from closing the door on him.

"You accused *me* of being a coward by refusing to recover," he said, holding the door ajar. "You said I needed to get on my feet and back to the land of living. Maybe it's time you took your own advice. Maybe it's time you stopped hiding from life and starting living again, too."

Firmly, insistently, he pushed the door the rest of the way open and entered her room. Elizabeth scrambled back, but Kristian marched toward her, fierce and determined. "Being with you is good. It feels right and whole and healthy. Being with you makes me happy, and I know—even if I couldn't see before—it made you happy, too. I will not let happiness go. I will not let you run away, either. We belong together."

She'd backed up until there was nowhere else to go. She was against her nightstand, cornered near her bed, her heart thundering like mad in her chest.

"You," he added, catching her hands in his and lifting them to his mouth, kissing each balled fist, "belong with me."

And as he kissed each of her fists she felt some of the terrible tension around her heart ease. Just his skin on hers calmed her, soothed her. Just his warmth made her feel safe. Protected. "I'm afraid," she whispered.

"I know you are. You've been afraid since you lost your parents, the year before your coming-out party. That's why you married Nico. You thought he'd protect you, take care of you. You thought you'd be safe with him."

Tears filmed her eyes. "But I wasn't."

He held her fists to his chest. "I'm not Nico, and I could never hurt you. Not when I want to love you and have a family with you. Not when I want to spend every day of the rest of my life with you."

She could feel his heart pounding against her hands. His body was so warm, and yet hard, and even with that dramatic scar across his cheek he was beautiful.

"Everything I've done," he added, tipping his head to brush his lips across her forehead, "from learning to walk again to risking the eye surgery, was to help me be a man again—a man who was worthy of you."

"But I'm not the right woman—"

"Not the right woman? *Latrea mou,* look at you! You might be terrified of marriage, but you're not terrified of me." His voice dropped, low and harsh, almost mocking. "I know I'm something of a monster, I've heard people say as much, but you've never minded my face—"

"I *love* your face."

His hands tightened around hers. "You don't bow and scrape before me. You talk to me, laugh with me, make love with me. And you make me feel whole." His voice deepened yet again. "With you I'm complete."

It was exactly how he made her feel. Whole. Complete. Her heart quickened and her chest felt hot with emotion.

"You make sense to me in a way no one has ever made sense," he added, even more huskily. "And if you love me, but really can't face marriage, then let's not get married. Let's not do anything that will make you worry or feel trapped. I don't need to have a ceremony or put an expensive ring on your finger to feel like you're mine, because you already are mine. You belong with me. I know it, I feel it, I believe it—it's as simple and yet as complicated as that."

Elizabeth stared up at him, unable to believe the transformation in him. He was like a different man—in every way— from the man she'd met nearly three months ago.

"What's wrong?" he asked, seeing her expression. "Have I got it wrong? Maybe you don't feel the same way."

The sudden agony in his extraordinary face nearly broke

her heart. Elizabeth's chest filled with emotion so sharp and painful that she pressed herself closer. "Kiss me," she begged.

He did. He lowered his head to cover her mouth with his. The kiss immediately deepened, his touch and taste familiar and yet impossibly new. This was her man. And he loved her. And she loved him more than she'd thought she could ever love anyone.

Kissing him, she moved even closer to him, his arms wrapping around her back to hold her firmly against him. His warmth gave her comfort and courage.

"I love you," she whispered against his mouth. "I love you and love you and love you."

She felt the corner of his mouth lift in a smile.

"And I don't care if we get married," she added, "or if we just live together, as long as we're together. I just want to be with you, near you, every day for the rest of my life."

He drew his head back and smiled down into her eyes. "They say be careful what you wish for."

"Every day, forever."

"Grace Elizabeth…"

"Every day, each day, until the end of time."

"Done." He dropped his head and kissed her again. "There's no escaping now."

She wrapped her arms around him, reassured by the wave of perfect peace. "I suppose if you're not going to let me escape, we might as well make it legal."

Kristian drew his head back a little to get a good look at her face. "You've changed your mind?"

A huge knot filled her throat and she nodded, tears shimmering in her eyes. "Ask me again. Please."

"Will you marry me, *latrea mou?*" he murmured, his voice husky with emotion.

"Yes."

He kissed her temple, and then her cheek, and finally her mouth. "Why did you change your mind?"

"Because love," she whispered, holding him tightly, "is stronger than fear. And, Kristian Koumantaros, I love you with all my heart. I don't want to be with anyone but you."

**From the magnificent Blue Palace to the wild
plains of the desert, be swept away as three
sheikh princes find their brides.**

When English girl Sorrel announces she wishes to
explore the pleasures of the West, Sheikh Malik
must take action—if she wants to learn the ways
of seduction, he will be the one to teach her....

THE DESERT KING'S
VIRGIN BRIDE
by Sharon Kendrick

Book #2628

Coming in May 2007.

REQUEST YOUR FREE BOOKS!

2 FREE NOVELS
PLUS 2
FREE GIFTS!

YES! Please send me 2 FREE Harlequin Presents® novels and my 2 FREE gifts. After receiving them, if I don't wish to receive any more books, I can return the shipping statement marked "cancel." If I don't cancel, I will receive 6 brand-new novels every month and be billed just $3.80 per book in the U.S., or $4.47 per book in Canada, plus 25¢ shipping and handling per book and applicable taxes, if any*. That's a savings of close to 15% off the cover price! I understand that accepting the 2 free books and gifts places me under no obligation to buy anything. I can always return a shipment and cancel at any time. Even if I never buy another book from Harlequin, the two free books and gifts are mine to keep forever.

106 HDN EEXK   306 HDN EEXV

Name	(PLEASE PRINT)
Address	Apt. #
City	State/Prov. Zip/Postal Code

Signature (if under 18, a parent or guardian must sign)

Mail to the **Harlequin Reader Service®**:
IN U.S.A.: P.O. Box 1867, Buffalo, NY 14240-1867
IN CANADA: P.O. Box 609, Fort Erie, Ontario L2A 5X3

Not valid to current Harlequin Presents subscribers.

Want to try two free books from another line?
Call 1-800-873-8635 or visit www.morefreebooks.com.

* Terms and prices subject to change without notice. NY residents add applicable sales tax. Canadian residents will be charged applicable provincial taxes and GST. This offer is limited to one order per household. All orders subject to approval. Credit or debit balances in a customer's account(s) may be offset by any other outstanding balance owed by or to the customer. Please allow 4 to 6 weeks for delivery.

Your Privacy: Harlequin is committed to protecting your privacy. Our Privacy Policy is available online at www.eHarlequin.com or upon request from the Reader Service. From time to time we make our lists of customers available to reputable firms who may have a product or service of interest to you. If you would prefer we not share your name and address, please check here. ☐

HP07

HARLEQUIN *Presents*

We're delighted to announce that

A Mediterranean Marriage

is taking place in
Harlequin Presents™—
and you are invited!

Leon Aristides believes in money, power and
family, so he insists that the woman who has
guardianship of his nephew becomes his wife!
Leon thinks Helen's experienced—until their
wedding night reveals otherwise....

ARISTIDES' CONVENIENT WIFE
by Jacqueline Baird
Book #2630

Coming in May 2007.